Tom Morton is the author of seven previous books, including the whisky travelogue *Spirit of Adventure* and the critically acclaimed novels *Red Guitars In Heaven* and *Guttered*. He is a past winner of a Bank of Scotland Press Award for his newspaper columns, and still writes regularly for the BBC website and for *The Shetland Times*, where his 'Nippy Sweetie' feature has become a local scandal. He presents BBC Radio Scotland's weekday afternoon show from its production base in Aberdeen and his home in Shetland.

Tom Morton

The Further North You Go

The Shetland Times Ltd.

The Further North You Go
Copyright © Tom Morton
ISBN 1 898852 95 2

First Published by The Shetland Times, 2003.

British Library Cataloguing-in-Publication Data.
A catalogue record for this book is available from the British Library.

Printed and published by
The Shetland Times Ltd.
Gremista,
Lerwick,
Shetland, ZE1 0PX.

Contents

Through the years, a man
peoples a space with images of
provinces, kingdoms, mountains,
bays, ships, islands, fishes,
rooms, tools, stars, horses and
people. Shortly before his death,
he discovers that the patient
labyrinth of lines traces the
image of his own face.

Jorge Luis Borges

I should like to rise and go
Where the golden apples grow;
Where below another sky
Parrot islands anchored lie.

Robert Louis Stevenson

JIMMY FIVE WELLIES

JIMMY Five Wellies was making tea.

"Tea," he said, pronouncing it as "tay". "You have to taste it, or it isnae worth the water." And what Jimmy meant by "taste" was a flavour powerful enough to overcome four teaspoonfuls of sugar and a large dollop of Carnation Milk.

This was serious tea.

Dominating the tiny kitchen, which was uniformly brown, like Jimmy, from peat smoke, was an old Rayburn Royale range. Every spring Jimmy would painstakingly cut his peats from the last remaining bank on the Scraada croft, raising them and stacking them over the summer until a team of locals bagged the crumbly, coal-hard lumps and transported them home for him. And after the rum and the bannocks and the McEwan's red tins, Jimmy would make tea for them as well.

He had once talked me through the process, after I, gasping from a seared throat, had made some patronisingly complimentary comment on the quality of the drink which was causing my mouth to go numb and my guts to quiver worryingly.

"Never clean your kettle," he said. "Never wash your teapot. Only empty it. You need to let a teapot age."

The Rayburn was always lit, the big cast-iron kettle eternally steaming on top. When tea-making commenced, Jimmy would lift the kettle on to a single, blackened ring which was connected to a butane cylinder by a cracked rubber tube, and light the gas.

While the kettle boiled, Jimmy spooned what seemed like pounds of loose Nambarrie leaves into a battered and blackened aluminium teapot, already heated on the stove. With a great whoosh, he ran boiling water in, rammed the ill-fitting lid on, and put it on the gas ring. Then he boiled the tea for a good five minutes. The lid rattled, and I swear you could see the thin sides of the teapot flexing.

"Infusing, boy. It's an infusion, tea. Patience is all. All."

After boiling it was allowed to settle. Then came the pouring – no strainer; tea at Jimmy's involved compulsory leaf-chewing – and the addition of sweet tinned milk. There was no fresh option, and the neat, superheated tea would have stripped all the enamel off your teeth and possibly removed your gums altogether. Sugar, I had found, was advisable, if only for stirring to aid the cooling process. Afterwards, you didn't need to eat for hours.

I had gone to see Jimmy after maybe six months in Shetland, because I had heard in The St Rognvald Hotel bar that one of the abandoned crofthouses on Scraada might be for sale, very cheaply. There were always stories like that going the rounds, and life in the condensation-dripping caravan I called home was palling. There was fungus growing on my clothes. Every night.

The word was that an old house, still roofed, with a tiny patch of garden could be bought off Jimmy for oh, maybe as little as five grand. Five thousand pounds for a house? I had come from a city where that was a week's rent in some areas. For a flat.

2

"Old Jimmy Five Wellies," said the vast fisherman called Ernest, positively gurgling with Unst beer and Trawler Rum. "He never wears anything but wellies on his feet, du sees. He has an outside working pair, a good pair for special occasions he polishes wi' Cherry Blossom. An old inside pair and a good inside downstairs pair. And another set he sleeps in, but naebody's ever seen dem."

It was too good a story, and too cheap a possible source of accommodation, to be ignored. So I rode my motorbike from Grunnawick towards Eshaness, the spectacular peninsula at the north-western tip of the Shetland mainland, and searched out Scraada. I found Jimmy in residence, experienced a cup of tea, and, after an hour or so's conversational foreplay, was informed that he had just sold Da Villians, a semi-derelict house on the north of Scraada, for not five thousand, but one hundred pounds.

"To Zander o' Mellaness," he had mused. "Ach, he needed it to keep his feed blocks in. It's just over the dyke from the Mellaness croft. A hunnert is a good price, too. Plus the decrofting. And a quarter acre."

Six months later, a £150,000 Norwegian kit house was standing at Da Villians, which had a spectacular view over the Eshaness cliffs out to the North Atlantic. Zander o'Mellaness, fuelled by a senior job at the Sullom Voe Oil Terminal, had bought his site cannily. He used the stones of the old crofthouse to build a garden wall. Jimmy just shrugged. That was the way of things, his narrow shoulders said.

By that time I had become a regular visitor to Scraada. I had gained immunity to the tea, even if I hadn't reached the stage of enjoying the actual experience, benefiting from the blast of caffeine and tannins which made Starbucks espresso seem like brown babymilk.

The caravan was about a mile away, and I would drop in when I was passing, or lonely and fed up with the condensation of my aluminium residence, and in the mood for some reminiscences about Jimmy's days on the Salvesen whaling ships. He had sometimes spent entire winters in the Antarctic.

"We had rules, you know," he would say. "Never kill the pregnant mother, never take too many of the beasts, always leave enough to give us another season. Others weren't the same." He grinned. "And then, if you had any money left from the card schools, it was back hame for the summer. I would go after the seals, shoot a few hundred of them. Good eating, boy! And the skins were worth a fortune."

I would nod enthusiastically, wondering how various Greenpeace-supporting vegetarian pals back in London, with their plastic shoes and subscriptions to *Resurgence* magazine, would take to Jimmy. The tea would have killed them long ago, I decided. It was tea for carnivores.

I saw most of Jimmy's legendary wellington boots. The dirty outdoors working ones, the clean, polished indoor downstairs ones, folded carefully down around his ankles, and a battered pair he kept for going to the peat shed. But three pairs of wellies didn't seem too excessive to me, in the almost inconceivably wet climate of the Shetland Islands. By that time I had two pairs of my own. I never saw the legendary overnight wellies, though. Our relationship never got the point where I could have asked if he slept in his boots. And he was never in bed when I went to Scraada.

*** *** ***

They buried Jimmy, just as the peat-cutting season started. We did. I was there. I felt involved, by that time. Part of it.

Three months previously, he'd been found wandering in his pyjamas near the last Scraada bank, his old tushkar, or peat-cutter, in hand. But it was 2 am and early February, with the

4

ground frozen iron hard. He was blue with cold underneath the peatsmoke residues. No-one could get much sense out of him.

They took him to the care centre, fed him, cleaned him up, joked with him, listened to his stories, which tended now never to have proper endings. And they gave him tea made from cooled electric kettle water and cheap Co-op teabags, served in polystyrene cups. I visited him there, but the quick, determined movements, the smiling memories of the Antarctic whaling, the deft control over Rayburn, gas ring and teapot, were gone. He was oddly pink in the peat-free atmosphere, and wearing a strange pair of yellow wellies, like yachting boots, short in the leg. I said nothing about them.

We sipped gingerly at the mugs of weak, colourless liquid we had been given by one of the attendants. He looked at me, frowning.

"It's an... infusion," he said. "Patience is what you need. Lots of patience. Otherwise it's a waste. A waste of..."

"Water, Jimmy," I said. "A waste of water."

The funeral was all black suits and battered parkas, mostly men. The kirk was packed, and at the graveside, the minister had to battle with a buffeting wind, and a stray, nervous sheep. Afterwards, I joined the assembled crowd of relations, neighbours and friends in the bar of the St Rognvald Hotel. I had learned things during the service. The minister had referred to a wife Jimmy never talked about, tragically killed by a stray bomb during a German air attack on Sullom Voe, which had been a flying boat base during the war. A three-month-old daughter killed too. Lost, the minister said. Lost.

A Distinguished Service Order, gained while serving as a Royal Marine Commando. An age. Eighty-seven. I had never even thought of Jimmy as having an age. He had been part of the

5

landscape. Part of life. I felt the sting of tears at the back of my eyes, but blinked them away. It wouldn't have done at all.

Clutching a large Black Label, I bumped into Ernest, the vast fisherman who had originally pointed me in the direction of Scraada. It turned out he was Jimmy's nephew, twice removed.

"Aye, a fine funeral," he said, as if we had parted only minutes previously, and were old friends, rather than drunken acquaintances from months ago. "Me mam's a cousin, du kens. Was. You never got that hoose off old Jimmy, then? No, Zander's got his palace up there now, eh?" We drank, both nodding.

"He was buried with his wellies on, du knows."

"Really? But which... how many... I mean... not those yellow ones?"

"His night-time ones? No. He'd stopped noticing what he had on his feet towards the end. They were the only ones he had at the care centre. And he had no shoes. They tried to get him to take a pair, or wear slippers, but he wouldnae."

"So..."

"So, me mam had a rake around at Scraada, and found his best indoor pair, good black ones. And he was buried in that and his best Fair Isle, one his wife knitted. Still fitted. He looked fine."

Later that night, much later, Ernest and I were in a croft house kitchen not unlike Jimmy's, listening as a boy who couldn't have been more than 16 played a fiddle air so sad you felt your soul was being slowly and exquisitely flayed. We were all flying with alcohol, replete with salt mutton and bannocks.

It was late, very late, and then our hostess, Meena Walterson, Meena o' Burns, who was Ernest's mother, began to pass out mugs of tea. It was tea of the classic Scraada type, thick with condensed milk, the colour of severely abused engine oil. I drank it with pleasure.

6

"It's the infusion, Ernest," I mumbled, my lips nerveless and rubbery. "You have to taste it, or it's not worth the water."

Ernest nodded.

"Aye, maybe," he said. "On the boat, we all drink Nescafe."

I remember walking back to my caravan in the silvery half-light of the simmer dim, the absence of darkness in Shetland summers, and feeling both the melancholy absence of Jimmy, and, for the first time since coming to Shetland, the certainty that this was where I too would end my days.

Two months later, Meena Walterson sent Ernest to see me, and he took me round to Da Burns. There Meena, the beneficiary of Jimmy's will, told me how the Scraada croftland, 100 acres or so of rough hill grazing, was being rented out to two local crofters.

"Yon caravan's no place to spend another winter," she said, peering at me through curiously trendy rimless glasses. In that strange Shetland way she could have been any age from 50 to 70.

"Tak' the Scraada hoose. Jimmy liked you fine. Rather than see it fall into a rattle o' shite." She had a forthright manner, Meena.

We agreed the same rental as I was paying for my decrepit mobile home. Not a pittance, but not bad. "No doubt you'll be wanting to do it up a wee bit. You'll manage that yourself, though." I agreed. "And you'll find Jimmy's tushkar's still there in the shed, if you want to cast some peats next year. Ernest'll show you how."

I would, I thought, like to keep Scraada's last peat bank operational. A kind of memorial.

Meena got up suddenly, her clumpy brogues rattling on the lino. She was moving towards the Rayburn.

"Tea," she said firmly.

CARAVAN CLUB

MAYBE you've been on holiday in a caravan, and had a really good time, perched on some Breton sand dune for a sun-drenched fortnight of barbecues and blistered skin. Perhaps you have happy childhood memories of towing a Sprite Muskateer or a Bessacar through France behind the family Vauxhall Cresta.

Even if nowadays you detest caravanners for their snail-like perambulations along the highways and byways of Britain, preventing your much swifter 16-valve progress, deep down maybe there's a germ of nostalgia for the hiss of Calor Gas in china clay mantles, the whiff of damp sponge rubber mattresses. Escape. Possibility. Freedom.

None of this applied to me. I had never been in a caravan before I arrived in Shetland, which has possibly the least trailer-friendly climate in the world, outside the Arctic Circle. Not that we're that far from the Arctic Circle here. Close enough for occasional severe discomfort, when the big gales come sweeping south, and the wind-chill strips the skin from your face.

Nevertheless, there are hundreds of caravans, statics, mobile homes, trailers, call them what you will, scattered across the rock and bog of the isles. Some, long abandoned as human residences, are inhabited by hens or sheep, their moquette cushions foul with heaped excrement. Others have been twirled and birled by hurricane gusts, dumped on their sides or casually picked up and dropped by the wildest of winds. Crumpled like bad tin toys discarded by some bored infant .

Others are holiday outposts of islanders' lives, places to leave behind the office job in Lerwick and stare at the sea and the sky, dreaming of the boat south, or north, or simply away. And some are year-round accommodation for the poor, the desperate and the transient. Which just about summed me up when I moved into Da Van, as it was universally known.

I had never felt terribly strongly about caravans. Being a convinced, not to say convicted motorcyclist, they had never been much of problem in the overtaking stakes. If anything, I felt a twinge of pity for the poor sods who were forced, like turtles, to carry their own shelters with them, for the housewives who never escaped the domestic drudgery of cooking and cleaning.

I had been a hotel fan ever since I could remember. "Hootels," I'd called them, as a middle class, only child, reared, spoilt in the clean, well-lit affluence of a Dunstable suburb. Later, grown and with the wherewithal or expense accounts to indulge myself, I became a connoisseur of hotels, from boutique city hideaways in Paris to gloriously fading country piles in Norfolk. The starchy crispness of clean sheets, the joy of room service.

Caravans, in the end, were for losers.

"Fine view, fine view," said Dodie Two Hats, jangling keys in the lock of Da Van. "Those rocks are the Hasta Stacks, 200 feet high the tallest one. A Grunnawick man once climbed the big one – Hasta Braalie – for a bet, oh maybe a hundred years ago. When he got back down, he found he'd left his pipe at the top. So he climbed up and again and got it."

I grinned into the bleating, scouring clifftop wind.

"I'm not much of a climber, Mr Ewenson. I'm just looking for somewhere quiet I can stay."

"Ah well," said Dodie, "some folk'll do anything for a smoke, you see. And there's no problem here if you want to smoke. Plenty of smokers have stayed here." He opened the door, and a swampy miasma of foetid, Capstan Full Strength air mixed with dampness and old, bad, fried food hit us both. I tried not to gag. "Could do with a wee airing. Minimum lease, three months."

Dodie was inside. I could hear his shoes unpeeling themselves from the glutinous carpet every time he moved his feet .

"Warm as toast, this is. Good Calor fire. And you can put on the cooker if it gets really cold. Well. You buy your gas from me. Only from me. There's a meter too. Takes pound coins. You'll find it's a fair rate. Considering the location. A view like that no money could buy. Not a king's ransom."

"How much?"

"Now then…" Dodie's face, flat and battered, shrank with cunning. He was all spectacles. "That depends. Are you on the broo? Will you be wanting a rent book and that? I don't mind, but it's, you know, a different rate."

"Cash," I said, "monthly in advance. But I'll buy my own gas." No doubt there was a rip-off built into the electricity meter. I was damned if he was going to do me on propane too. There was a silence. Dodie was not used to tenants with ready money.

"Ah well. Now then. How about, ah… well… a hundred?"

"A month? You'll be registered with the council as a landlord? The caravan will be passed safe and all that, I presume? By the Environmental Health or whatever?" For a second or two I was enjoying the deal-making, the sparring. But then the spark died, and I was bored with myself and my stupid hustling ways. "Fifty a week, how about that? No receipts."

"Ah well. . ."

He was right. The view was extraordinary. So was the smell. I pulled out a wad of cash, counted out three hundred pounds, and held it out. Five weeks' rent. He didn't take it. Hands in pockets, Dodie half-smiled at me.

"Now then. You should be careful, carrying all that money. People, certain people might become a little excited by the idea of it." I smiled at him.

"That's all until next month. I took it out of the bank specially."

"Ah. A bank." As if the idea of such a modern contrivance was a matter of wonder. "There's no telephone, not nearer than the Grunnawick Post Office. But you'll have one of those mobile things, won't you. They're a godsend here." And he pulled from his pocket a state-of-the-art Nokia, glittery and chromed. "It's a good to keep in touch, I think. As they say. People can always find you, these days. No-one's ever able to escape the constant, as I might put it, hurly burly of life. All right, let's say 60 pounds a week. And the gas, I think you'll find is more, well, reliable from myself."

He had me sussed. My Ericsson was lying at the bottom of the North Sea, and the name I'd given him was, I realised belatedly, hardly calculated to defuse curiosity. John Smith, I'd said, in as natural a way as possible. Like the late leader of the Labour Party. He'd glanced at me blankly, but there was a glint of amusement and cunning behind those glasses.

"Eighty, and I'm not here."

"I never saw you, Mr Smith. Not at all. Unless I'm emptying the meter, I won't. Or bringing you your cylinders." I peeled off some more notes and handed them over.

"And, eh, £30 in advance for the gas. It is a large cylinder, you see. It will last a while." Longer than you, he was saying. Longer than you, you soft English bastard.

I paid. Paying was what I did. I was here to pay.

Of course, Dodie didn't keep his word. He told everybody he came in contact with everything he knew about me. Fortunately, that was very little. But there was no anonymity in Shetland, no isolation. Eighty quid and I'm not here, I'd told him. But I was there. Here. A real person in a real place. Wherever it was.

Whatever I was.

Da Van was the last remnant of an entire clutch of caravans which had been sited on a field near Grunnawick. They had been bought and concreted solidly into place by Dodie Two Hats, one of the peculiar breed known as crofterpreneurs.

His real name was George Ewenson. There was another George Ewenson, his third cousin, called Dodie Pee, who hated Dodie Two Hats with such a fervour he had once been arrested for urinating into the back of his relative's Morris Minor. It was unfortunate for him that a policeman had actually caught him in the act.

"Ach," Dodie Two Hats had allegedly commented. "Plenty of sheep have pissed in there already. An old goat's pee won't make no difference."

Anyway, the Grunnawick Holiday Park had made Dodie Two Hats (the name was supposed to refer to his multiple business activities, but I always saw it more as a comment on his conniving, yet oddly appealing nature) a fortune, first of all from the construction phase of the Sullom Voe Oil Terminal back in the 70s, when over 10,000 men arrived in the islands to work, play, raise hell, make and lose huge quantities of money.

When they left, Dodie Two Hats, racking his brains for ways of attracting a large lump of replacement tenants, contacted desperate accommodation officers at councils and mental hospitals. Soon some highly unusual characters were planted in the rain, mud and darkness of Shetland winters. And more cash was filling up Dodie's pockets.

Two Hats had never actually obtained planning permission for the site and he was given a week to remove all the vans. Most were too decrepit to save, so he simply hired a digger and driver, excavated a pit and bulldozed them into it. This had been a classic Shetlandic method of waste disposal since the arrival of heavy earth moving equipment. One van he moved to his croft and let out to unsuspecting holidaymakers. The other he sited on top of a cliff near the Hasta Stacks, lashed to the concrete blocks with some rusty steel cable, and rented to the sad and desperate.

And to me.

I was his perfect target market. Even having cash and a false name wasn't that strange. Drug dealers, absconding bigamists, pathetic fraudsters, lost fathers; all passed through Dodie's hands.

"That Two Hats," said Mel, the Shetlandified English barmaid at Grunnawick's St Rognvald Hotel, fount of all knowledge. "He's weird. In a funny way, he thinks he's doing these people a favour. It was the same with the loonies. He's sort of kind. I mean, the rents are a scandal, but then he'll give them Christmas presents. He'll lend them money. Fix their heaters at midnight. But he honestly sees what he does as a social service." She grimaced, black eyebrows flickering beneath the dyed blonde hair. "I think he means well. No matter what you might hear."

But to tell the truth, that hadn't been much. Everything I heard came through Mel or whoever else in the St Rognvald deigned to speak to me. And if Dodie was weird, I was clearly weirder.

Mel had graduated from the Grunnawick Caravan site. To one unit of a small council house clutch called Slocka, built with

13

oil money in some architect's idea of what was traditional crofthouse style. On acid, presumably. It was a higgledy-piggledy clutter of soaring terraced rooflines and suburban pebble dash.

The tenants ranged from psychopathic drunken malcontents to calm, happy, settled families with steady incomes, whose aspirations were to get some land and put up a Norwegian kit house. Like Mel. "Doing a Fjogstad," it was called. You could see Mel poring over catalogues showing these wooden palaces, dreaming of triple glazing. She had a kid, too. A baby, really. I didn't know who the father was. Lost, somewhere along the line, no doubt. Mislaid.

It was late February when I moved into Da Van, and the weather was so bad I found it funny. Maybe hysterical describes it better. The steel cables holding the trailer to its concrete retainers thrummed in the biggest storms, while the windows were glazed white with salt. Some days it never got light. Dodie duly provided the gas, and neither it nor the electricity was as fraudulently expensive as I'd feared. I cleaned, bought food at the Grunnawick shop, and bit by bit saw my anonymity vanish. Or at least, my isolation.

The first inkling was when the library van stopped outside my door one twilit morning and hooted. I went out to meet a grinning, blue-eyed earth mother of about 60, wearing a Fair Isle kaftan. I was struck dumb.

"John, it'll be" said this vision in flapping knitwear. "I'm Carrie the Library. I was just passing by, and Jeanie at the shop said you had moved in, and you were a young, educated, kind of cultured fellow. I thought I'd see if you fancied ... anything to read. Literary sustenance."

Her accent was pure Tyneside. "Crime, perhaps?" There was a long pause.

It was not, I felt, a suggestion for a novel I might enjoy. It

14

was a query as to what dreadful misdemeanour had brought me to Da Van, to Shetland. I smiled my most disarming public relations tooth-revealer.

"Carrie. I'd be delighted. I was just thinking I could do with something to pass the time."

Carrie came every fortnight. I always made sure I was in to receive her, hand back my books and borrow more. Make clear that a shag was out of the question. And tell her as little as possible. She began knocking at the door, rather than hooting, and then just opening the door and shouting: "Yoo hoo, John! It's me!"

All the time her eyes would flick around the caravan, searching for gossip fodder. But I kept the walls bare. And my conversation expansively empty. I'd always been good at that anyway.

I walked in the half light of the day. I rode my motorbike into Lerwick sometimes. And I spent a lot of time at the St Rognvald, talking to Mel, and the people I came to know as Victor, Alf and a businessman called Alastair. There were others, silent, fleeting presences: Angus of Brinnishaader was pointed out to me. Someone called Steph The Creel, a man, like many Shetlanders of indeterminate age. He could have been anywhere between 40 and 80. It was curiously calming.

I was fine, really, I told myself. Fine. Recovering. Nobody asked me where I came from, though I volunteered the fact that I had stayed in London for a long time. They just welcomed me and waited, and watched.

I slept well in the caravan at first, despite the noise of the wind, the clatter of hail and rain on the aluminium roof. Then one night I woke in a curious silence, and found myself getting out of bed, and obsessively checking the gas cooker and the old Cannon heater.

People suffocated in caravans; the thought kept hammering

15

at my brain. I had a bottle of Montepulciano I had found in the Coalfishreek Co-op. I opened it and drank half, leaving my heart palpitating painfully and a sour wine migraine reverberating in my head.

Gas. I was sure I could smell gas. I leaped out of bed, hauled on my old Drizabone coat, a pair of cheap black wellies, and sploshed out into the frigid wetness of an uncharacteristically still night. The valve on the big red propane cylinder was switched off. Firmly.

I always left it on.

Maybe I had switched it off and forgotten. No. Not a chance. I had never thought much about the gas, apart from comparing Coalfishreek prices with Dodie's (20 per cent mark-up; not bad). I cooked, flicked on the heater. That was it.

I went back to bed and slept. Dreamlessly. Next morning I went outside to switch the gas back on. It was a beautiful, clear, crisp twilit morning, like a sunset in reverse. The light would last, oh, maybe four hours. And the gas was already on.

Madness. I had feared some kind of insanity ever since leaving London, and now here it was. Full throttle mind loss. That day, I had been mumblingly asked by Steph the Creel to come out with him and lend a hand hauling lobster baskets, if the weather was fine. It was, and I went, glad for the skin-shredding cold of the sea, the abrasive tearing of wet salt ropes on my hands, pulling the creels on board, reaching for the deep, dark blue lobsters with rubber bands to halt the clacking of their claws.

I avoided going back to the caravan that night, crashing at Steph's after he cooked a huge fish tea (coalfish, or piltock, the heads stuffed with oatmeal and accompanied by an enormous quantity of Aquavit Steph had procured from some illegal Danish trawler). I understood barely a third of what he said to me. But he was kind. A kind man.

16

When I returned to Da Van, the gas was as I'd left it.

There was no smell inside. I checked the weight of the cylinder to see how full it was. There was plenty of propane there.

Nothing happened for week or so. Then again, in the middle of the night, this time a howling, rain-battered one, I woke up again. I could hear something amid the racket outside of the van. It was a steady, rhythmic clink-clink-clink.

I got out of bed and switched on the light, looking for the sound's source. It was the gas heater. The clink-clink-clink was the electric flint which lit it. It worked when you pressed a button on the side of the fire. Except I wasn't. Nobody was. After a few seconds of wakeful watching, it stopped.

I didn't sleep again that night.

Next day I called on Dodie Two Hats in his mansion of a house and said I was concerned about the gas system, that I thought there might be a problem with it. He said nothing, just gazing at me.

At last he spoke: "Ah well," he said. "I have another caravan I could maybe let you have. Not such a good view, right enough, but nearer the Post Office. And it's by the Sands o' Swarthoull, not up high. Not maybe as exposed. I could maybe let you have it for, well now. The same price."

So I moved to another of the Grunnawick Caravan site's redistributed units, this one slightly less battered in fact than Da Van had been. It was known simply as Swarthoull. It rocked a little in the winds, but the gas never misbehaved.

"So you've moved," said Carrie the Library, when she came banging on the door of Swarthoull a fortnight later. I was bleary eyed and hungover after a night in the hotel, surviving a surprisingly twangy local country band called The Long Gone Lonesome Daddies but who were, Steph informed with surprising, devastating wit, better known as the Shag Anythings.

"Yes, Carrie," I said. "problems with gas up at Da Van."

"Ah," she said, looking solemn. "There always were problems with the gas in that particular van. When it was on the site at Grunnawick, three workers from the site were gassed in there with carbon monoxide.

I flinched. Suddenly the Shetland morning looked evil and threatening.

But Carrie was smiling.

"Och, they were all right. They didn't die. The bus arrived to take them to Sullom Voe, and their mates hauled them out when they couldn't wake them. After ten minutes in a wee breeze they perked right up."

"Perked up?"

"Oh yes. You'll maybe fancy this new James Ellroy I have in? You liked his last one, about how his mother was murdered. Didn't you, John?"

Sighing, I invited Carrie inside.

I told Mel the story and she looked at me with a grim expression.

"Ghosts," she said.

"No, Mel. Ghosts are related to dead people. Those three guys didn't die, according to Carrie." She snorted.

"Carrie! Bloody historian, is she? Comes up here with a lagger from the site and sleeps with every crofter who can sow a turnip! The literary lover. I'm surprised she hasn't made a pass at you, John."

So was I, kind of. Carrie had restricted herself to double entendres which had gradually vanished from our conversation as she'd got to know me. Or maybe my erotic spell had worn off.

Steph was drinking sweet black and tans in the corner of the bar. He was the only other drinker there.

"Du's weel oota it," he said. "Weel oot." And nothing more.

A week later Da Van exploded. It was empty at the time. Dodie hadn't been able to rent it out.

"Ghosts," said Mel. "You had a warning. Somebody up there must like you."

"Nobody died, Carrie," I said. "And nobody up there likes me even slightly. If there is anybody there."

*** *** ***

Three months after I moved into Scraada, a young man arrived at the hotel, dwarfed by one of those gigantic hiker's backpacks. His name was Peter, he said, and his dad had raved about Shetland so much he'd had to come and see it for himself

"Your dad?" said Mel as I sipped a pint of Orcadian Raven ale. The boy was drinking lager.

"Yes. He was a contract worker at Sullom Voe in the seventies. Lived in a caravan. In fact, he and his mates were nearly killed in it."

"Carbon monoxide?" Mel flashed a glance at me.

"That's right. They thought Dad had recovered, but he had terrible asthma afterwards. Took him off finally last year. Before he ever had a chance to come back here." He smiled. "I can see why he loved it. It's beautiful."

"When did. . ." But I stopped Mel asking the question with a flick of my glass. Beer spilt over the counter.

"I'm sorry to hear that, Peter" I said. "What was it your father did at the terminal?"

He took a sip of his lager, and turned to me. "He was safety officer at the fractionation plant," he said. "Where they separate out the gas from the oil. Funny thing was, gas was his bread and butter, so to speak. He lived and, well, he breathed it."

I bought Peter a whisky with his pint, and together we toasted his father's memory. I felt it was the least I could do. Steph was in, and I bought him a sweet black and tan.

"Du's weel oota it, boy," he murmured. "Weel oota it."

19

Dear Billy and Jerry,

I am sending this to your mother, who may
destroy it. I know, or think I know, that
there are other letters to you she has torn
up or burnt. She was probably right. They
were written when I was drunk and maudlin,
sorry for myself, racked with guilt.

Now, I'm just drunk. Drunk and scrawling.
But I mean it. Mustn't talk like this,
write like this about your mum, though.
Respect. That's the thing. Respect. R-E-S-
P-E-C-T, that is what you mean to me...
Aretha. Goddess run to fat.

They were probably written to her as much
as, or more than you. Those letters. Maybe
this is too. Actually, I'm not sure if I
will post this. Too drunk. Too much
disrespect. Maybe I'll do that film thing,
lodge it with the bank, lawyer, something.
To be opened in the event of my death. Sent
in the event of my demise. OK then...

So. Without wanting to be dramatic, this
is the last time you will hear from me. I
felt I had to tell you. Will have heard. Is
that the tense? Past imperfect. That's me!
Imperfect. And in the past. Just had a
large whisky, to keep my nerve up. Spirits
up.

So anyway, your mother may want to keep
this as a souvenir. I know you're reading
this, Dorothy. I wish I hated you, Dorothy.
I never did. Still don't. Hate myself for

not loving you any more, maybe. Take this
as a sign that one part of her life, your
life is over. Your life, her life. Proof
that it's over. I am.

I left. You know that. I rode away and
left you. But I had already left you,
abandoned you, as is normally said of
fathers. As in he pissed off. He left them
in the lurch. I'm not denying that. I'm not
proud of it.

The last leaving was different. I think
you knew that too. But then, I'm a selfish
bastard who only sees my own point of view.
His. There's a song, actually, Randy
Newman. Great songwriter, brilliant. Irony.
That's what he does best. Irony.
Ironically. And he wrote a song about, from
the point of view of, inside the head,
actually, a father who's about to piss off.
And he pats his little boy on the head and
says: "I just want you to hurt like I do,
honest I do, honest I do, honest I do." And
he's a self-deceiving sanctimonious
bastard, ladling out his pain on his
unsuspecting children. Child.

I had no idea where I was going. Or
rather, I did have an idea. What I was
going to do at least. Just not where.

I wanted to say sorry. I wanted to say
goodbye. I wanted — I want — to take myself
out of your lives forever. For good. For
your good.

But that's crap, isn't it. It's for my

21

good. It's all about me, really. How I feel. How I don't feel. And that's the thing, boys. The not feeling. That's what really scares me.

I left your mother, left you because of me and what I wanted. Or to be as precise as I can, at least in this state - fuzzy more than drunk. Necessarily fuzzy - I wanted more than the life we had as a family. Or was it actually wanting, so much as just taking? Taking what was there, what was on offer. Being unable or unwilling to say no? Or just too pissed to say no?

Morality, boys, let me tell you, is the art, the pain of choosing what is right. Excuse me while I have a cup of coffee. Instant.

Choosing what's right. Whatever that is. Thing is, I stopped choosing. I let myself be chosen, by circumstance, by women, by drugs and alcohol and money and third-hand fame. I was adrift and at first, it was great. There's a tremendous release, a joy in that. In that lostness. Forgetting. I forgot you. I left you behind...

It's like all those stories about being in a forest. Hansel and Gretel, all that. The forest at first is an adventure, fun, a delight. Then night falls, and it's still cosy, fun, and adventure. Till you wake up cold and shivering, and begin trying to get back home. That's when the brambles start ripping your flesh, and the paths back

close up, or turn into a confused, blind
maze.

Your mother. Dorothy, I shouldn't have
done those things, said those things. Boys,
It shouldn't have happened that way. I
wanted the best for you. And she did too.
She finally realised that wanting the best
for you meant wanting the worst for me.
That was her decision. I suppose me turning
up pissed and stoned to take you out to
Burger King that time was the last straw.
Confirmation. However many times it was.

Can I tell you about the pain? The pain
that came before this weird, sickening
numbness? The pain I caused, and the pain I
felt? No. It sounds wheedling, weak. In
fact maybe all of this does. Just want you
to hurt like I do.

It's over now, anyway. Or will be soon. I
wanted to tell you though, that I loved and
love you, and wanted the best for you. I
know that must sound sick, sickeningly
hypocritical, and you may well ask how I
can say that I love you when I don't feel
anything. I don't know. I don't know how I
know.

I can only say that I know I do. Love
you. And maybe that's a kind of morality
creeping in at the last. Knowing without
feeling. What can I call it. Big words, big
words...drag them out. Certainty without
emotional confirmation. And I did once love
your mother. I did, Dorothy, I did love

you. I did. We loved each other. The damage
I have done to her is irreparable, and now,
so is the damage I've done to myself. And
to you. All of you. All of you.

I'll be dead. That's the notion of this.
The purpose. You won't read this until that
has been proved, and I will make sure that
there's no dubiety. There won't be some
unidentified body lying unclaimed for
months. I'll take myself out of your life
and leave you to heal.

I'm going now.

Goodbye,

Daddy

MAALIES, MOOTIES AND MUCKLE SCARFS

WHEN I first came to this part of Shetland, with its single-track, isolated roads running by jagged voes, miniature fjords of dark water, I couldn't understand why so many smashed and broken sea shells were lying on the rough grey tarmac.

The birds do it. Sea birds, herring gulls, known locally as maas, and great black-backed gulls, swaabies. They pick up shellfish and drop them on a hard surface to break open the shells. Then they gobble up the soft, squelchy internals.

It's the kind of thing that might catch on at some ultra-cool London eatery. Smash your own scallop by dropping from our convenient mezzanine. Free champagne if you hit a waiter.

Some people come here for the birds alone. The night-loving storm petrels, mooties; fulmars, or maalies and the cormorants and shags – scarfs and muckles scarfs – which were harvested during the war and served in ultra-cool 1940s restaurants as North Isles Pheasant. Enough to make a vegan birdwatcher puke up his muesli.

Shetland is twitcher central, a birdieperson's paradise. And even the locals can be obsessed with all things feathered. They have wonderful, resonant names for all of them. A black guillemot is a tystie, an eider duck a dunter. And an arctic tern, my favourite, with its streamlined, swallowesque beauty, its aggressive defence of eggs and young, and its annual trips from Shetland to the Antarctic and back: tirrick, they call it. Tirrick. Exactly the noise it makes, a kind of electronic clicking, a gibbering bleep.

I didn't know or care anything about Shetland's wildlife. That wasn't why I'd come here. Birds? I wouldn't have known a twitcher from a nuclear scientist. Or that they were sometimes the same thing.

But my fellow escapees, the refugees and battered human flotsam washed up on these northernmost lumps of Britain, include a lucky few who combine their obsessions with isolation, with sheltering in some form of safe haven: I'd heard about a supposed Bosnian Serb war criminal in Fetlar who lived only for a glimpse of a snowy owl. The daughter of a famous American politician who spends every waking hour whale watching. The son of a well-known, if somewhat dead, modern composer who spent his summer's counting gannets on the island of Noss, and his winter playing very bad banjo with a local cajun group.

And me? What am I doing here?

I'm here because there's nowhere else after this. This is where you run out of Britain and the British. Where you fall off the edge. Ultima Thule, the Romans called it, supposedly. The Edge of the World. Local folk call Shetland The Old Rock. And it is a rugged piece of landscape, no doubt about that. Treeless, for the most part. Infertile. Unsheltered, you can find yourself cowering beneath the biggest skies you've ever seen, in some of the wildest weather.

Or maybe you've been dropped here, on the hardness of the place, like some whelk, scallop or mussel. Smashed and laid open, raw and exposed to merciless predators.

26

The birds, so gleamingly attractive in glossy guides, and in the minds of bird watchers, can be horrible too. Vicious. My first week or so in Lerwick didn't prepare me for the avian life of the North Mainland. I rode the bike out of town for my rendezvous with Dodie Two Hats, and into an Alfred Hitchcock movie.

Bonxies. Big brown skinhead football hooligans of the skies. The stories they tell about bonxies would scare the living daylights out of Richard Attenborough. The great skua, as it is properly called, will attack you. Not normally hitting you, although there are lurid tales of people killed by having a beak penetrate through the eye. I met one of the local twitcher supremos in a Lerwick pub, and according to him, bonxies only collide with you by accident.

"It's only if they misjudge the distance that they actually clobber you," he said. "They're just trying to frighten you a bit. Because you're too near their nesting site." On the other hand, the bastards will kill other birds for food they might be carrying – including the mighty swaabie – and will go after lambs if they're feeling particularly hungry. Or indeed, so the story goes, babies left out in prams. I mean, one minute you're offspring's gurgling happily next to the washing line, the next he's a meal for a roving feathered terrorist.

Life in the wondrous Shetland Isles, eh? And there are more bonxies here than anywhere else in the world. At least we don't have sea eagles any more. They used to carry babies off to their nests before eating them.

"I did have one death," mused my twitcher pal, "definitely caused by a bonxie." Oh really, I wondered into my pint. "Yeah, it was on Noss. I was leading a party of visitors, and there was this man, he was kind of… well, elderly. He wandered off, and when we went back to the boat, he wasn't there. Old. Not doddery, just past his prime. We found him lying in a bonxie

27

colony, stone dead. Heart attack. Hadn't been hit, or anything. The birds had scared him to death."

Bird presence around the first of my palatial caravans was extensive. A tirrick colony on the shingle beach below the cliffs, and fulmars. Knowing little about birds at this stage, apart from to avoid bonxies, I was unprepared for a maalie spouting the smelliest substance in the world all over me as I ventured out for a walk during my first morning in residence. At high velocity. The smell — like rotting fish crossed with skunk, was appalling. It took days to get it off my skin, and the rather nice Berghaus fleece I was wearing simply had to be dumped.

The tirricks peeped and chirruped like mad mobile phones, buzzing and beeping around me in a desperate, not threatening manner. I kept away from their shingle-laid eggs, watched through binoculars for them to hatch. I felt for them, envied their loyalty, their dedication to breeding, raising, protecting their young.

The desperate, gene-bred stickability which saw them making that incredible annual journey to winter in the Antarctic, and back to Shetland in spring.

And yet I kept eyeing the sky nervously for a bonxie – a Mig to these Spitfires – thundering at me with the deadly, kamikaze accuracy, intent on killing me stone dead. Bonxies like eating baby tirricks.

My first inclination, when faced with these airborne terrors, was to run. But I had given up running. I had nowhere left to run. So I learned to cope.

I didn't fight them, or wave things at them. I spoke to Mel at the St Rognvald Hotel. Mel told me about a famous female photographer who arrived in Shetland to snap the sea parrots, the puffins – wonderfully named tammy nories, locally – which you never see unless you teeter on the edge of cliffs or go out on a boat.

The photographer, miles from any form of civilisation on the uninhabited west side of North Roe, in unusually wonderful, hot weather, found herself attacked by a determined bonxie with, apparently, a snack of human flesh on its mind.

The woman was wearing a sarong, and came up with the panicked, if somewhat bohemian notion of taking it off and waving it above her head to distract the birds. Which may have been a reasonable enough idea. If she'd kept hold of it. But she didn't. A gust of wind caught the wildly-waved scrap of cloth and wrenched it from her hand, gauzily fluttering it out to sea.

All would have been well, I suppose, had she been wearing knickers. But she wasn't. And the resultant explanations to Peter o' Da Lees and his wife Joanie, who lived in the first house she came to were, to say the least, interesting. They grew more and more interesting as they were relayed across the North Mainland. Becoming, years later, the stuff of legend. Peter o' Da Lees, who was in his eighties when this happened, died not long after. Joanie apparently always blamed the shock of answering the door to the naked photographer.

I had no sarong, and I waved nothing. I merely erected a new washing line on the other side of Da Van. I retreated, really. Tactically. All right, technically, I ran.

If in doubt, move. It seems to be my nature.

Not that I've become a birdy person in my time here, but sometimes you can't help taking an interest. A red-necked phalarope is a thing of beauty, and a snowy owl just looks like a big, airborne ghost. But it's the waifs and strays that get me, the strange visitors swept off course that shouldn't be in Shetland at all. A pair of black swans turned up a fortnight ago, not from Australasia, at least not directly, but escapees from a widlife park in Sweden. Yet to see them preening themselves on the Loch of Nibister, like Victorian Ascot hats come alive was… strange.

It hit me on a deeply emotional level, despite the presence of more than two dozen twitchers who had flown in from the south to add them to their life-lists.

The swans were visitors, just passing through. Strangers blown way off course, and quickly on their way again.

Not like me. I'm more like Albert Ross, the albatross, the poor, benighted, utterly solitary albatross who used to appear on the island of Unst every year, mateless, old as eternity, waiting and watching on his cliff ledge. Everyone here loved Albert. His arrival was announced on the local radio, featured in *The Shetland Times*, the weekly newspaper. He came year after year. And then he didn't arrive. Presumably dead, having searched in vain for a partner. For a life. I just keep thinking of Tennyson and hope some drunken bastard didn't shoot him.

Just a week after arriving here, I was staying in the hostel in Lerwick, drinking in Captain Morgan's, and I was invited to a party in Tingwall, a village which passes for one of the capital's suburbs. There I met a girl, who was maybe 20. Half my age. I never found out her name. We talked, the drink easing my wariness, my sense of my own absurdity, until I found myself stumbling onto one of favourite pick-up lines from the old days. The quite recent days, to be honest, but they seemed old. Ancient. So did I.

"Reflexology," I said. "I used to have a girlfriend who was a trained reflexologist. She taught me how." That's all you had to say. It rarely failed. This girl picked up her foot and slammed it into my lap.

"Go on then," she said.

Her foot was bare, and beautiful, fine boned in that youthful way. Unbattered by the weight of life. Good nails, too. I could feel my lips twitching. But her big toe seemed oddly shaped, bent slightly and enlarged; her other toes were very long.

"I'm from Foula stock," she said. "Du kens... you know,

Foula? The island out east, 20 miles or so off. Biggest cliffs in Britain. Nearly. St Kilda's maybe bigger."

"You have lovely feet, I mumbled, nervously pressing at her heel, which was amazingly soft.

"Och, shite," she said, smiling a beautiful, 19-year-old smile. Did I say she was 21? God knows what age she was. "I've got Foula feet. The men used to climb the cliffs in their bare feet, to get at the shags."

I knew what a shag was. Neither a dance nor the sexual act; a smaller cormorant.

"They used to live on the birds and their eggs. Solans. Gannets too. And they say the men's feet changed shape over the generations to cope with climbing. Foula foot. And I've got Foula feet. Though I never climbed a cliff in my life. Go on then. Reflexology, please, Mister Cockney Rhyming Slang. Gertcha, mate!"

But I couldn't. I left the party, walking back through the cold winter darkness into town, until I was picked up by a bunch of drunken fishermen heading home after a two-week stint at sea. They unloaded me with what they called a fry, a bin-bag full of assorted fish I had no idea how to gut, and left drunkenly outside the hostel. I staggered to bed for a sweaty, heart-poundingly uneasy sleep.

I was wakened next morning by a violent, tremendous screeching. Outside the sky was full of gulls. All tearing at my abandoned bag of fish and at each other. The hostel warden, a strange little man called Patrick, shook his head when I went down to the kitchen to make some coffee.

"Somebody left a bag of fish out there, and look what's going on. There'll be shit everywhere." He eyed me. "It wasn't you, was it? I thought I heard somebody come in late."

"No," I replied, "absolutely not."

"At the fish factory, they have a good scheme," he said. They

31

take a fish, and put a lighted banger, you know, a firework in it. Then throw it in the air. The birds are so excited they just gulp it down. And a second later, they explode." He laughed uproariously. "I've seen it done with razor blades, too. Birds," he said. "They're vermin."

I sipped bad instant coffee which wouldn't properly dissolve. My head felt like there were razor blades in there, chopping the cerebral cortex into slurry. The screaming outside was harsh and metallic. You could hear the fluttering bang of wings on windows.

"Oh, I don't know," I said. "Birds are all right."

THE TRIUMPH OF ALKAVIR RADFURGEN

I KNEW, vaguely, about Up-Helly-A', the Viking fire festival.

If there had been a picture of Shetland in my mind before coming to the place, it would have been bearded men in skins and horned helmets, burning a boat. I hadn't realised that dozens of such flaming eruptions of dressing up and drinking took place every year, from the northernmost tip of remote Unst to the famous, or infamous Lerwick affair.

Most are bits of community fun, with one squad of men and women dressing up as vikings, more or less, and the other locals forming so-called squads that tour around three or four township halls on the night, performing skits and then tearing into whatever drinking and dancing is on offer.

The Lerwick Up-Helly-A', though, is on a huge scale, organised like some kind of royal pageant and involving dozens of massive parties held in halls, hotels and houses, at which over 1000 men – and it's all men, no women allowed – strut and perform, having previously paraded the streets, sung lustily and burnt a full-sized Viking galley. And, I was told in the Staney Hill Hostel when I arrived in Shetland, there was sexual licence of a kind unseen since the days of Nero or Freddie Mercury. The sanctity of marriage is suspended for 24 hours. Only 24 hours, I thought. Why not a lifetime?

"Fir da Vikings, onyway, da jarl squad, as we caa them," said Jeemsie, in one of his rare sober moments. He was forever being thrown out of the hostel, and then marched back in by a team of police and social workers, to whom he was a bit of a favourite. "All da wimmin are abandoned by their husbands, du sees, and go to the dances demselves. So when they see some stranger in a Viking outfit, or maybe some neighbour they've had the hots fir, weel, it's aff ootside and aff wi' da knickers. 'We axe fir what we want.' Dat's the jarl squad's motto. And for 24 hours, naebody's supposed to refuse them."

Well, I thought, that's what being a Viking's all about.

Nothing refused, on pain of raping and pillaging. Or semi-inebriated, semi-consensual sex.

"What about all the other men, the ones in ordinary squads?"

"Ah, dey dress up as everything du could imagine.

Animals, women – lot of men in Shetland like to dress up as women, du'll find. And sometimes dey get lucky too. Maybe some girl's had her eye on a man for years, and then he turns up at the party's she's at, da hall, and Bob's yer uncle." Jeemsie grinned slyly. "Or, if you're no careful, your faider."

It was, I thought, pretty much your standard Roman Saturnalia, or a New Orleans Mardi Gras, or any number of festivals worldwide where the darkness of winter and the coming of fertility were celebrated with drink and shagging. Soho on a Saturday night.

The Lerwick Up-Helly-A' is held, always, on the last Tuesday in January, and was clearly unmissable. A man in the Thule Bar sold me a ticket for dance at the Shetland Hotel, and that evening I did my best to make myself presentable before heading out for the Hillhead, the road at the top of the town, near the town hall, where I had been told the great parade of guizers began. Lerwick was more than crowded. It seethed with people in the darkness, and there was babble of excitement in the clear, icy air. Brass bands played as hundreds of men gathered in phalanxes, led by a troupe of Vikings in costumes which glittered in the sodium lights. Their enormous and enormously phallic axes looked entirely genuine. How could a maiden refuse such a fellow? Bravely, perhaps.

They surrounded what looked like a life-size Viking war galley, complete with a dragon's head at the bow. The lorry wheels it rested on kind of spoilt the effect. Other men were dressed in furry tiger suits, dresses, bizarre bits of rag and leather. All carried staves of wood, each with a bound sackloth bundle at one end. There was a strong smell of paraffin. Then the street lights went out, and as a firework soared into the air, exploding with an enormous bang, a violently purple light erupted from a flare, illuminating the Vikings crouched around it, like some psylocybin nightmare.

In seconds all the torches were lit, and as the brass bands struck up again, the men began to march and sing: something about grand old Vikings and ocean waves. It was hard to ignore the spindly legs, straggly near-beards and protruding Adam's apples of some less than fully developed Norsepersons. Behind me, an English voice was commentating, loudly: "Started with burning tar barrels, young men engaged in bloody criminal vandalism, if you ask me. They would throw the barrels into the shopfronts of people they didn't like. Ancient business though.

"Up-Helly-A' means the lightening of the year. Signified the start of spring. Went all romantic after the Second World War.

"Middle classes took over, everyone started having real beards for it, not joke false ones. Now it's a bloody religion."

The marching went on. And on. My feet froze, and I began to wonder how the Vikings were coping, in their windblown skirts. Perhaps they wore fur underpants. Finally, the entire gathering of torchbearers paraded into a town centre swing park, and formed a ring around the stationary longship. There was a silence, then the grand old Vikings on the ocean wave stuff began again.

Flaming staves started looping through the air into the dragon boat, which caught instantly. The night turned flickering yellow and red as the men sang, and I occasionally glimpsed the outline of winged Viking helmets against the flames. For a moment, the whole thing transcended kitsch and my own dull cynicism. I felt a weird tingle run up my spine. But it could have been a melting hailstone. Ferocious squalls of stinging hail were now sweeping through the town.

I had a half-bottle of Stewart's rum in my jacket pocket, and as the flames began to die I unscrewed the cap and let the warming spirit rasp down my throat. I almost choked as something hard nudged me in the small of the back.

"Here, any chance of a wee nip?" It was a Shetland voice, male and slurred. The speaker was a diminutive Viking, no more than five foot tall, but arrayed in the finest glinting brass armour and a helmet with raven's wings. The lack of a beard and the presence of black-framed Buddy Holly glasses was a little disconcerting. I handed him the rum

"Can't see a thing without these specs," he muttered.

"Almost had a disaster, a bloody disaster at the turn down from the Hillhead. Couldn't see where anyone was supposed to be going." He took another sizeable gulp of spirit.

"Shouldn't you be… aren't you burning the galley?"

"Ach, no. Been the jarl in the past. My time's over. Now I'm just a glorified traffic warden, directing the drunken bastards so they don't set the toon on fire." He smiled suddenly, revealing a shiny set of teeth which glinted yellow in the firelight. "Shortest guizer jarl in history, me. And the first without a beard for half a century. Wanted me to wear a falsie, but I said, nah. Too scratchy. You never know what's lurking in a beard. Beasties. Infections. Won't have it on any o' the staff at the sewage works. Have a bloody drink, why don't you?"

I said nothing about the rum being mine in the first place, but carefully avoided offering my new Norse friend any more. He grabbed it out of my hand anyway, took a long gulp. Well, he was a Viking. It was his night. I was merely a civilian, up for pillaging. Or being pillaged.

"Got to go to the Shetland Hotel, help sort things out there. Wife's sister's one of the hostesses. Could see it far enough. Had my day with this Viking lark, really. I'd rather be at home wi' the telly and a few red tins. I'm Manson, by the way. Charlie. But you can call me Vaam. Everybody else does. Sewage man, that's me. Waste disposal executive, they call me, but I'm just sewage through and through. Vaam. It's Shetland for smell. Smelly. Even though nobody has more showers than me. Smells nicer. Cleaner. I emptied Harry's bloody shop of Davidoff Cool Water. I can take a laugh, I don't mind. But not Wee Vaam. Smelly's all right on it's own. But no' Wee. I don't like that."

I suppose if I'd been called Charles Manson, the nickname Smelly might have been just about acceptable. I could see why he didn't like being called 'Wee'. Suddenly the whole episode seemed vastly amusing. Here I was, sipping rum from the bottle with a man called Vaam, but definitely not Wee Vaam. Even though he was the Wee-est Viking in Up-Helly-A' history, and apparently proud of it.

"I was Alkavir Radfurgen, du kens. When I was guizer jarl. Every one takes the name of a great, great warrior viking. I was Alkavir, It means Harrier of the Red Farmers. Alkavir Radfurgen. That was me. For a day. Twenty-four hours, and then it was Vaam again. Don't you even think of calling me Wee Vaam, by the way. I know I'm wee, but that's my privilege. Big in other ways if you get my meaning. No complaints in that regard."

The crowds were drifting away. I decided to abandon my rum and make a bid to escape.

"Sorry, Alka… Charlie. Vaam. Got to get going. Nice to have met you. Maybe see you later on at the Shetland Hotel."

"What, you won't even have a drink?"

But I was already scurrying towards the network of narrow, incredibly steep lanes that lead down to the waterfront. Why were so many Scottish ports built on sheer cliffs leading down to the sea? Defence, I supposed, my woozy, rum-laden brain spinning lazily. On the flagged central throughfare of Commercial Street I pushed open the door of Da Noost, a joint which was, in truth, well and truly jumping. I ordered a pint of export and let the crowd suck me in.

After a couple of hours I fished out my ticket and wandered down to the pier to get a taxi for the Shetland Hotel, a vast modern toilet wall of a place out near the ferry terminal.

The function suite on the top floor was easy to find. You just followed the trail of slumped bodies, couples in mid-orgasm and empty bottles. It was as if some kind of mid-seventies rock'n'roll orgy was in full swing, only involving men dressed as Teletubbies and Cabbage Patch Dolls. And Vikings of course. Like a Led Zeppelin after-show thrash crossed with a convention of children's entertainers.

I stepped over an apparently dead Viking on my way past the bar. Another warrior downed in the battle with the demon booze. One fist was closed tightly around a red tin. I leaned in close to see if he was breathing. He was. The evidence was in the excruciating smell.

There seemed to be a localised earthquake underway in the St Catherine's Suite. After about five minutes cowering next to the door, I realised it was nothing more than a mass Boston Two-

Step, propelled by a six-piece dance band featuring two accordions and amplified to brain-melting proportions. It was like listening to Jimmy Shand with Motorhead helping out. Through Limp Bizkit's PA system.

Men dressed as moulting lions cavorted with satin-clad sylphs, some of them female. I remembered Jeemsie's comments about Shetland men liking to dress as women, and I wondered if some of the outfits on display had come from the back pages of *Exchange and Mart*, that typically British trade magazine, the ultimate source for transvestism in all its daft paraphernalia. A crushed Viking helmet, its raven feathers moulting, lay at a crazy angle beneath a beer-stained table. I became aware of a noise below and to the left of me, and something tugging at my sleeve.

It was inevitably, Wee Vaam.

"How's… how's du?" His Shetland accent had increased and roughened. In his hand was a full bottle of Trawler Rum, the main rival to Stewart's in Shetland. "Have a drink, you bastard." He smelt strongly of burnt hair and wool, and seemed a bit singed all over. Maybe I hadn't noticed it earlier on, what with the general fieriness of the event.

Just then a tray of flaked brown meat was shoved under my nose by a harassed looking middle aged woman in an off-the-shoulder evening dress.

"Here boy, ait some reestit mutton. Damn you, Vaam, leave the lad alone. He's no' wanting to end up a dribbling wreck like dee. It's wonder du's no in da hospital after dy antics."

I nibbled at a piece of the meat, which was initially delicious, tender and moist, but then incredibly salty.

"What happened, err… Vaam? Did you hurt yourself?"

"Na, na. Never du mind. Just par for da course. It'll make dee drink, that stuff," he dribbled, his accent changing. I noticed odd black marks on his hands, and his arms were blotchy and red. Drink, probably. "Try da soup. It'll line dy gut."

Another bustling lady, also dressed up to the Freeman's mail order catalogue equivalent of the nines, summarily thrust a polystyrene cup into my hand. In it was a thick, lumpy, khaki-coloured substance. It was salty too, and delicious. I ate and drank, feeling somehow energised and sustained. And then very, very thirsty.

"Beer," said Vaam. "Du needs beer. Pit oot da fire." And he was right. I did need beer.

Much of what happened during that evening, that night, the following morning, is only a vague memory. There was lots of drinking, and eating. More soup. More salt. Liquid in various alcoholic strengths. I danced reluctantly. As far as I could tell, all the women I danced with were exactly that. Women. The room spun. But somehow the magical combination of soup and salt meat kept the worst of the drunkenness at bay. Some kind of old Viking tradition, perhaps. Alas, or fortunately, no-one propositoned me. But kindness and hospitality seemed to be the order of the night.

And besides, I still had the cold of my long motorcycle ride buried deep in my bones. At least that's what I told myself. From the waist down, I was ice to the core. Maybe I'd be that way forever.

But I smiled, tried to flirt. It was as if all the women instinctively realised I shouldn't be pursued, like some scarred or branded wandering soul: a beggar, fool or subnormal wretch you were nice to, but couldn't take seriously. Or take.

I didn't mind. To give up the sanctity of marriage for 24 hours, you still had to believe in it. The sanctity, that is. And I didn't. Hadn't.

I remember being served a breakfast of bacon rolls and scalding coffee, sprawled beside Vaam, who had somehow dented his Viking helmet and spilt soup down his tunic. At least I hoped it was soup.

"What I want," he kept saying. "What I want is. . ." But we never quite reached whatever that was.

I was preparing to make the long walk home, gritty behind the eyes, but remarkably sprightly considering the alcohol consumed and the salt doubtless erasing all kidney function. Vaam levered himself up on his elbows and regarded me with a rheumy, baleful glare.

"What I want is a Viking funeral. That's all." The woman who had first given me the reestit mutton came hurrying up.

"Du's an aald fool, Vaam. Poor lad has had tae listen tae dee all night." She peered up at me. "Will du get hame all right?" I smiled. My face felt tight and roughened, as If I'd been in bad weather. "Home or somewhere," I said. "Wherever that is."

*** *** ***

A month later, already haunted and obsessed by weather, home was a juddering caravan, and I knew the vibration was being caused by at least a force nine wind, gusting to violent storm force 11 ("some structural damage may be caused" said the laconic coastguard leaflet which explained the Beaufort Scale) when the door to the caravan flew open.

I put it down to the ridiculous wind, until a figure clad in fluorescent yellow oilskins wedged itself through the narrow entrance.

"Ho, Johnny boy!" it said, deluging the worn and sticky carpet with second hand sleet.

"Alfred," I replied cautiously. You never quite knew with Alf, a salmon farm worker, whether he was going to sob uncontrollably on your shoulder or hand out a severe nutting. I

41

had seen him do both within the space of ten minutes at the St Rognvald. To the same person.

"Why's du here, boy? Why's du no' doon da bar, waiting for the procession tae start?" Look at the weather, I thought of saying, look at the sheep flying sideways up the voe. But that would be nonsensical to Alf. Bad, awful, even apocalyptic weather for him was a given, something you had to deal with, and in most cases ignore. But then, if you were having to take a small boat out in near-hurricane conditions to feed salmon, I could see that any nervousness on my part about leaving a caravan for the comfort of a bar might seem a little, well.

Typical, perhaps. Cowardly English bastard.

The aroma of Old Holbourn tobacco… peatsmoke, fish and used beer began to fill the van. Alf was a single man of between 30 and 60. Telling the age of some Shetland males and for that matter females could be a problem. Especially in the remoter areas, there were people who at the age of around 30, assumed the appearance of someone twice their years, and never altered until genuine decay made change inevitable. The women would thicken and coarsen, adopt the hairstyles and clothes of their mothers and grandmothers, while the men, in their perennial blue boiler suits, battered and burnished by weather, would only by infinitesimal degree show a deepened wrinkle here, a whitening beard there. I had high hopes that I would find my ageing processes arrested by bad weather and dark rum, but so far, it wasn't working. My face, despite the application of Nivea moisturiser – I was probably the only male north of Lerwick using it – was beginning to look like a Barbican down-and-out's or a loser parliamentarian's, all broken veins and permanently red nose.

Still, it was early days. Maybe dark rum was an elixir of youth which just took a little time to kick in.

"Du's coming to Up-Helly-A', though? At the Grunnawick Hall? Everyone'll be dere. You canna miss it."

I hadn't planned to. One Up-Helly-A' was enough for one year. And after the size and spectacle of Lerwick, I was, slightly embarrassed at the thought of how Grunnawick's little effort might look. Tawdry and daft. And anyway, I wasn't feeling like company. I wanted to chill in my own blank, icy self-pity for a while. As you do. As usual.

"Alf, I think I'll just stay in. Got to watch the caravan in this wind. I mean, I don't want to come back and find it gone, do I?"

Alf looked at me with utter incredulity. "Wind? This is just a wee breeze, Johnny. No, du isnae stayin' in by deeself, moping aboot whatever du's moping aboot. Come on. I have da truck ootside."

There was no escape. Within minutes, muffled in my newly-purchased Dickies canvas parka, I was bouncing along in the passenger seat of Alf's Toyota Hi-Lux, along with the various tools, bits of rope, dried fish and what looked like a leg of mutton. Old mutton.

"That's not... reestit mutton there, Alf, is it?"

"Whit?" He peered down onto the floor as we careered along the single track road at horrifying speed.

"Nah, dat's no reestit. Yon's just rotten. I'd forgot that was even there. It'll do for Mitnie's pigs."

Still not looking at the road, as he steered with apparently magical ability, Alf asked: "Does du like reestit mutton, eh? I must give dee some. Special recipe. Soaked in salt and salt petre, dried ower peat, left for twa years."

Two years?

He began peering through the opaque, sleet-lashed windscreen again.

"I had some at the Lerwick Up-Helly-A'. It was... soft. Salty but soft."

"Ah, that would hae been in the soup. Du'd get soup wi' it. Good for the drink. That an a bannock. Du'll get plenty o' that tonight. Whit time is it?"

I looked at my cheap plastic Timex. "Just coming up for half six."

"Shite! We'll just hae to get straight to the burning pool. They'll be setting aff for da march any minute."

"What do you mean, pool? Isn't it like Lerwick? Don't they have a galley on wheels?"

"Nah. Here they have a real galley. Float it oot onto the Loch o' Grunnawick. Ca' it the Burning Pool. Do must hae heard it?"

And I had. The Burning Pool. Had never thought to ask why it was called that.

*** *** ***

There were dozens of cars and trucks already parked along the shore of the little loch about half a mile east of the Grunnawick township. I could see a wavering line of flames approaching from the west, and as Alf parked and switched off the rattley old diesel, the sound of the same song I had heard in Lerwick came and went in the howling of the wind.

"No night for man nor beast," said Alf.

"Just Vikings."

Alf rummaged in the old Toyota's parcel shelf, and produced a bottle of Stewart's Spiced Rum. "Here. Warm deesel'." I did.

Gradually, the sound of wavering singing grew louder. And finally the procession arrived at the Burning Pool. As Vikings went, they were all right for a dark night, but nothing like as convincing as the ones I'd watched in Lerwick. They did appear to be having a better time, though despite the cold. There was a lot of shouting and grinning. And drinking. There were women,

44

too, sort of Vikingesses. And the same assortment of furry animal costumes I'd seen before.

The Norse galley at Grunnawick was a good bit smaller than the Lerwick one. Not so much a longship as a shortship. But in the glare of headlights and the flicker of flames, it still looked impressive.

"Dey spend a whole year building it," muttered Alf." I was in da jarl squad one year. Fine business. Woke up two days later in a fishing boat off Orkney."

"How did…"

"Ach, it was to do with a dog. A sheepdog. I'll tell dee anither time. Look."

They were launching the galley onto the turbulent waters of the loch, the Burning Pool.

"Dere's a cable, tied to the back o' a Landrover on the idder side," said Alf. "It just gets pulled into the middle o' da pool." And sure enough, the galley was sliding into the water.

The assembled throng of gale-battered Up-Helly-A' enthusiasts began throwing their torches towards the little longship, which bobbed up and down a few yards from the shore. Many seemed to miss, but it wasn't long before the boat was on fire. As it lit the wind-tossed, eddying water, the sheets of hail and sleet, and outlined the little crowd of Vikings and gonk-like figures on the shore, the scene became cruder, more powerful, more elemental, less ceremonial than the big, self-important Lerwick equivalent.

Suddenly there was a commotion, and what appeared to be some sort of struggle, followed by a splash. Alf was opening his door, and getting out. Vicious blasts of icy weather battered me.

"Ah Christ," shouted Alf, his voice buffeted by the wind. "That'll be Vaam, the bastard."

I got out and followed him down to the shore line. Two bedraggled and very wet Vikings were hauling a small figure out of the water. In the firelight, I recognised my companion of those rosy Up-Helly-A' hours in Lerwick. Wee Vaam. Charles Manson, Waste disposal executive. Mr Sewage.

"What the hell's he doing here," I shouted in Alf's ear.

"Ach, da bloody same. Always da bloody same. Get's pished as a fart, then comes tanking down an' tries ta throw himself onto the galley. While it's blazin'. Course, he's so rat-arsed he canna see it properly, and he thinks he can throw himself into it, and it's actually the water. Then everybody gets soaked hauling da prick oot."

Vaam was not dressed as a Viking, but in some kind of cotton track suit, as if he'd been in training. Someone was holding a bottle of Trawler to his lips. Wet and freezing as he was, Wee Vaam was smiling.

"All I want is a Viking funeral," he shouted suddenly. "All I want. I'm a dying man! Let me end my life in a blaze of glory!"

"Crap," said Alf in my ear. "There's nothing wrong with the bastard except too much rum. Drives his sisters mad. Tries to jump on every burning galley at every Up-Helly-A' he's capable of getting' to. Did du see him at this year's Lerwick Up-Helly-A'? Cunning. Or more pished than usual. Waited until the fire died doon a wee bit, while the guizers were just beginning to turn awa', then made jump into the embers. Just as well as the fire brigade was there anyway. Hauled him oot."

I remembered the odd, blotchy scarring on Vaam and the odour of ash and smoke I'd smelt at the Shetland Hotel that night. Presumably he didn't die because, like those firewalking New Guinea tribesmen, he was in some weird ecstasy. Or so pissed nothing affected him.

"Bloody Hell. Does no-one…"

"Tolerance, Johnny Boy, tolerance. Live and let live. It's Shetland you're in, no Devil's Island. He has twa or tree sons, does Vaam. But they've given up on him. Had to, really. When he's pished, any rate. He's a lost soul."

*** *** ***

There was plenty of tolerance evident at the Grunnawick Hall that night, as post-Up-Helly-A' partying accelerated through the night and into the early hours of the morning. Tolerance of terrible skits by wandering, inebriated squads. Tolerance of bad dancing, much of it by me. Tolerance of everyone by everyone.

Wee Vaam was there, of course, veering between paralytic drunkenness and more or less joyous dancing, flirting and the muttering of nonsense to whoever he could corner.

"A Viking funeral," he said to me at one point. "'S'all I want." Well, quite. Alf told me that Vaam had driven up to Grunnawick on his own, and would quite probably drive back home to Lerwick in the morning.

"Luck of the devil, that little bastard," he said. "Never caught by the cops, not once. Or never arrested. Probably in the bloody masons, too. That's why they never let him burn at all these Up-Helly-A's he goes to."

"How did it start?" I was taking a respite from the more or less continuous Boston Two Steps and Eightsome Reels, carried out with brutal energy.

"Och, just the drink. He was jarl at Lerwick, and that was the first sign something was wrong. Before they burn the galley, the jarl stands in it and waves his axe aboot. Vaam wouldn't get out. Had to haul him doon, in the end, with him yelling about wanting to go to and join his bloody forefathers."

"So he took it seriously?"

"Aye. Well, you could say that. He was already on a bottle of Stewart's dark a day by that time. Must be worse now. How he manages to drive I don't know. Sewage plants runs itself, of course. Everyone turns a blind eye."

47

"Well," I said, smiling through the brown fizz of McEwen's Export, "I expect it's a question of tolerance, Alf."

*** *** ***

Wee Vaam's luck ran out on the way back to Lerwick. God knows how he was able to get into his car, let alone drive it as far as the hamlet of Videroe. Anyway, like many a drunk before him, he misjudged the tightening bend on the way out of the village, rolled the car through the fence and down the hill, where it lay on its roof for about 30 seonds, witnesses said, before catching fire. It was a Citroen BX, much of it made of plastic, and it burned fiercely, there next to the voe, that Saturday morning.

They found a few sticks of bone, apparently, but basically there was nothing left of Wee Vaam at all. Of Charles Manson. Or Alkavir Radfurgen. The alcohol residues probably helped him burn.

The turn has always been infamous in Shetland, since they built the new road. It has a name, taken from the croft about 100 yards to the east. It's called Valhalla.

They had a proper funeral for him, of course. It was in *The Shetland Times* announcements column, soberly recorded, Church of Scotland. There was probably a coffin, carried by the sons. It would have been a short one. And light. There's no crematorium in Shetland. Wee Vaam might have appreciated that final burning. But what would have been the point, as Alf pointed out to me at the St Rognvald, many weeks later, of burning the wee bastard twice?

BEFORE

"DAD, don't go ."

He was smiling. A strained grin. As if somehow he had to prove he was good, he was happy, he'd be no trouble. He would cause me no pain, no problems, if I only stayed. But I was almost shocked. I knew the words had been dragged out of him. They weren't characteristic. He was a sullen, pubertal fan of Rage Against The Machine, Marilyn Manson and And You Will Know Them By The Trail Of Dead.

"It's up to you dad, but…" The smile was slipping. His shoulders hunched. Childhood slipped once again beneath the hard shell of adolescent disdain.

His younger brother was not smiling. He was biting his lower lip, frowning fiercely at his feet. We were standing outside a newsagents and confectioners, just around the corner from their mother's house. Their house.

It was Christmas Day. The shop was shut. And the house was closed to me.

I'd given them cash-stuffed envelopes. Hugged them. Had the hugs shrugged off. And then we'd gone for this bitter walk. And they were cool, cool with me, cold, but cool too about what

49

Christmas had in store. Granny was coming. Dinner was in the oven. Yeah, OK.

But dad wasn't staying. Dad didn't stay, these days. Hadn't for a long time. What they didn't know was that dad was going away properly. For good. Or maybe they did. Maybe that's what broke through Billy's studied indifference.

I told them. Told them I was leaving town.

Where, they wanted to know, unexcited. I said I didn't know where I was going. Because I didn't. I had left them once. And now I was leaving them again. It was what I did. I was getting good at it.

"See you then, Dad. Can we head home now?" Cool. The preservation of the cool. The birth of the cool. Why was 'cool' good anyway?

"OK boys. Let's take you home."

Let me take you home. To your home.

She was standing at the front door, waiting. I tried to kiss the cold cheeks of the boys at the gate. Connected briefly with Gerry. But Billy brushed past me. They didn't linger, throw their arms around me, cry or plead, as I might have half-hoped. They went inside, into the aroma of food and spice, love and family. She just looked at me. Merry Christmas, everybody.

The bike looked like a sick joke. A male menopause in plastic and steel. This is what you exchange it all, for, throw it all away for, then? Some pathetic *Easy Rider* dream of escape? Throw what away. There's nothing here for me.

I unlocked the helmet from its security bracket, took the gloves from the topbox. I felt nothing. I had stopped feeling any thing a long time ago. No sorrow, no excitement, no hint of road romance. No relief. No guilt at fucking up the kids' Christmas. If I had. I pressed the starter and the flat twin fired immediately, clattering, staccato.

And then I left.

SANTALAND

SANTA came to Grunnawick in July, when the days were long and Shetland was basking in a heatwave. If, that is, Shetland can actually bask. It is not a basking sort of place, The Old Rock. It crouches, gloweringly, with a vague twinkle in its rheumy eye. It huddles against the risk of winter, even in the midst of the simmer dim.

I hated the thought of Santa. Christmas. All that warm and cuddly family stuff. But I kept my mouth shut and listened. And watched. I'd never been in a bar with any sort of Saint Nicholas before. Any sort of saint. Any sort of Nicholas, for that matter.

So anyway Santa came to the St Rognvald Hotel, and booked in for three nights. He liked being called Santa, he said, but answered to Father Christmas as well. Or St Nicholas. Jokingly, of course. His real name was Justin MacTavish, which was an even more ridiculous name than Santa Claus.

"Upwardly mobile English mother," he said in the drawling accent of the would-be upper class. "Scottish father. Named me as a kind of mongrel, I suppose. Ho, Ho, Ho. You'll have another beer?" The entire bar assented. For three days, it was Christmas, Christmas, Christmas. Ho, ho and ho.

51

Not that Santa wore a red suit. He was a designer outdoorsman, all Berghaus fleeces, Timberland shoes and Gore-Tex jackets. Expensive stuff. And there was no luxuriant, Up-Helly-A' beard. Just a sort of overgrown designer stubble. Which, for that matter, was a dirty reddish brown, and not the accepted white.

"I'm your Santa, boys," he would grin over his Glenfarclas. "Apologies to any ladies present. I come to bring tidings of great joy."

"That," muttered Alf, "was an angel. As in the birth of Jesus."

Justin didn't turn a well-groomed designer hair.

"Angels. Did you know that the word has a technical usage? In the city?" His London drawl grated hard against the measured buzz of Shetlandic accents in the bar. "An angel is an investor, a source of financial input in any given venture. A rum to go with that, Alfred?"

Justin spent a fortnight in Shetland, based at Grunnawick, running about Northmavine in a hired Toyota Landcruiser with a notebook and, usually, various employees of Shetland Enterprise and the council's development department in tow. Notes and photographs were taken, councillors entertained. Birdy people were cultivated. Journalists from *The Shetland Times* and BBC Radio Shetland were given supposedly exclusive briefings; cautious stories appeared in the paper and were broadcast: Shetland was to host a major new development which would combine tourism, commerce and, well, mistletoe. Santaland was going to be built, probably in North Roe. Justin seemed to like North Roe

"Can't have the North Pole, after all. Can't be doing with it," said Justin. "Too cold. Too far away. They don't speak English. Or the approximation you bods do. Anyway. North Roe; North

Pole. Sounds pretty much the damned same to me. Far enough north for a two-day trip from London."

"And probably not so many desperate grant-making bodies," said Alf, slurred slightly, "at da North Pole."

"Have another, Alf," said Justin, genially.

The plan was for a kind of small Santa theme park. A resident Santa-alike would be installed, and gullible children, plus desperate parents would be flown in year-round to visit the bearded one in his, ahem, residence.

"We'll have reindeer," said Justin. "Maybe elves. Or fairies, maybe bring in some reindeer. Reindeer would do well here, I think."

I couldn't resist pointing out that, while Shetland in winter, and often in summer, might feel as cold as the North Pole, there was no certainty that the one substance most associated with Christmas would be present, at least in any quantity: snow.

"Ah, but there will be snow, at least around Santaland itself," Justin smiled proudly. "We'll use snow machines, like the ones ski resorts have. We will have guaranteed snow. Within a strictly limited area, of course."

Santaland would have an internet presence, it seemed, and would be a kind of call centre for children who wanted to make their requests of Santa. Bairns could write, phone, text or e-mail, and could be guaranteed a reply. A team of local folk would be employed, said Justin, as Elves and Fairies. Cash would flow. At a time when the rundown of Sullom Voe was becoming a threat to Shetland's longstanding economic security, this was catnip to the executives at Shetland Enterprise and the council.

Justin left with, it was reported in the paper, a grant from the development department towards the cost of preparing a business plan, and a promise from Shetland Enterprise that they would, once this was ready, employee a firm of consultants to carry out a feasibility study. Somebody picked up the tab at the

St Rognvald. No-one was quite sure who it was. But it wasn't Justin.

It was September when the consultants arrived, two sharp-suited young men who said they worked for a company called Insight Assessments.

"Oversight, more like," said Alf. "Or overspend."

"Overshite," mumbled Victor. Or something that sounded like that.

Gerald and Ernest, the two young men were called. They stayed in Lerwick, and made a flying visit to Justin's favoured Santaland location. This was an owner-occupied croft called Da Grunnings. On it, in a beautifully-appointed one-story house converted and upgraded by the charitable Trust, lived Johnny o' da Grunnings, who was in his late sixties, a retired policeman and a pleasant enough chap, though liable to drunken depression on occasion.

Johnny mostly kept himself to himself, which was just as well, as when he did mix socially, he was liable, and had been all his life, to getting into fights. He had left the islands as a young man to become a policeman in Glasgow, where his natural tendency towards violence and confrontation had saw him rise to the rank of Sergeant. Before being busted to the ranks for meting out some rough justice to a drunk who turned out to be a member of the same masonic lodge as his chief inspector.

He had returned to the islands of his birth, unmarried – no-one, it was said, would have him – when his mother had died, aged 103. And loaded. There were dark suspicions as to how he'd obtained the money.

"Got to expect he'll be around for a while, too," sighed Victor. "Runs in the family."

Johnny had fallen out with his neighbours, with the fish van man, with the shopkeepers in North Roe, Hillswick and

54

Ollaberry. Every week he drove into Lerwick, where he did a Safeway shopping and picked up supplies at Jarmsons. He looked after a token number of sheep – on his own; he had quarrelled with everyone who helped him at caa'ing, dipping and the like – and he was rumoured to drink large quantities of wine, which he ordered by the case from some mysterious southern source. Sometimes, braver youths would fire air guns at his windows or throw kale at his door. They stopped when he discharged a shotgun several times at random into the night.

How Justin had cultivated him no-one knew. Probably money had something to do with it. Gerald and Ernest, at any rate, received what seemed like a warmish welcome at Da Grunnings. They paid a desultory visit to the St Rognvald, Bought everyone a drink, asked a few questions.

"Consultants," I said to Victor. "Nice work if you can get it."

"Two grand a day, I hear" he replied. "That's a lot of ESAs."

"You could be an elf," I said, "in the call centre. In Santaland. Steady job. Free uniform."

"No. I want to drive the sled. I'm ower wee for an elf." True. He is only six foot five. But, as the *Lord of the Rings* movies showed, you can have largish elves. Look at Liv Tyler. My sort of Elf. Good Elf, as they say on *Eastenders*.

In late October, a story appeared in the paper containing liberal, and positive quotes from Justin, and a photo of Da Grunnings. An announcement was imminent, Justin said. Finance from " a number of sources" was almost complete, and the charitable trust had made "a tremendously generous offer to invest in what will be a crucial development for Shetland's long-term health and future". Grants of several hundred thousand were on the verge of approval by Shetland Enterprise, the story revealed. Insight Assessments had given the plan a green light. Agreement had been reached with the owner of Da Grunnings, Mr John Fergus Nicolson, and with the Crofters Commission for a change of use. Reindeer able to cope with the Shetland climate had been found near Aviemore.

"Christmas is a time of good will," Justin was quoted as saying. "I will come north this Christmas and I now hereby make a commitment that I will never leave. Shetland will be my home. The confidence invested in me by the various funding bodies will be repaid! Santa Claus is coming to town!"

The story also announced a search for three, ah, persons – women carefully not excluded – suitable for playing Saint Nicholas in shifts once Santaland was up and running. Over the next few weeks, a number of prospective Up-Helly-A' beards turned mysteriously white.

In the run-up to Christmas, I was busy. Keeping busy, keeping my head in the north, away from everything down there, an ocean and two lands away. Things went wrong. Maybe I'll tell you the story sometime. Maybe I won't.

Anyway, just before Christmas, in its festive edition, *The Shetland Times* announced that a joint statement had been received from the council, the charitable trust and Shetland Enterprise, indicating that Santaland Shetland Ltd, the company set up by Mr Justin MacTavish, had gone into receivership. Low-interest loans from the charitable trust and the enterprise company would be recovered, it was hoped. Once the bank that had provided Mr MacTavish with the money which had released the first instalments of the grant package had got its moolah back. Fat chance, mused an editorial. No-one knew where Justin had disappeared to. But for him, Santaland had become a big fat Christmas box worth several hundred thousand pounds. Even Insight Assessments, it turned out, was a front company operated by him at a distance.

The people of Northmavine are resilient, and they shrugged off the disappointment. All except Johnny o' Da Grunnings. It was on Old Yule, aptly enough, that he appeared in the St Rognvald, three sheets to the wind, and unnaturally talkative.

"Abominable," he spluttered into an ill-advised Crabbies Green Ginger. "Abominable. Abominable."

"What, Johnny," said Vic. "The Snowman? That might be a wheeze, eh? Turn Da Grunnings into the mysterious haunt of the Shetlandic Abominable Yeti, recently rediscovered."

"The abominable peatman," someone said. A look from Johnny silenced the laughter.

"My... my police contacts are still... I know people," he slurred. "I know bad people and good people. You needn't think that MacTavish is going to get away with this." He stumbled towards the door. "I was going to buy a house in Puerto Pollensa, you know." And he was gone.

None of the Santaland funders ever got their money back, of course. More plans for new and exciting Shetland businesses came to the fore. Luxuriously packaged peat in decorative Fair-Isle silk sacks for suburban homes; minke whale farming for the Japanese restaurant market ("mammalian aquaculture" it was called); the conversion of the entire island of Unst into a detoxification centre for alcoholic Norwegian businessmen; uranium mining in Sandwick; hallucinogenic mushroom farming in Yell. There were high hopes for all of them.

Justin MacTavish was found, in the end. It was summer by then, and he had been dead for six weeks. There were lurid stories from Santiago, the Chilean capital, where his body was discovered. One tabloid reported that he'd been alive when persons or persons unknown tied him up, broke his arms so he fitted, and shoved him up the chimney of the luxury villa he was renting. Quite far up. Because then they lit a fire. Apparently the smoke asphyxiated him. Some sort of bungled drug deal was suspected

"Always the problem with Santa's supposed entry down

chimneys," reflected Vic, over a pint of Old Rock at the St Rognvald. "The risk of jamming, suffocation or incineration."

He turned to Johnny o' Da Grunnings, whose mood had improved over a summer he had largely spent, he said, visiting old friends south. He had returned a markedly different person: cheerful, prone to visit the bar. We were, of course, also very frightened of him indeed.

"Can I get you a drink, Johnny?"

"Why not?" said Johnny. "Give me a glass of that red wine. The Chilean stuff. I've got this business idea you might be interested in. It's what this community needs, after all. Not inward investment. Something from the grass roots."

"Absolutely," said Vic. "What is it?"

"Well," said Johnny. "Have you ever heard of the Abominable Snowman?"

Dear William and Gerald

Sorry about this. I'm not dead. Surprise!
Just drunk. Not dead drunk. Just pissed.
Pished as they say hereabouts. Never mind
where. Never mind.

Couldn't go through with it. At least not
yet. Sorry. Still have the possibility.
Humans always do. It's the last resort, the
constant resort. Hope you're not too
disappointed.

Not fair. That one's for your mother, you
bitch.

Formal. Sorry for the formality. But
you're growing. Grown up. No, not grown up,
still my little boys. Bairns they call it.
Call you. Call them.

Why am I still going? Well, there's
nothing else, is there. Can't be. Kill
yourself because you've got nothing to live
for, and what do you get? Nothing. Nada. So
what's the point of that? Does that make
sense.

Sorry about the spill. Mark on the paper.
It's rum. Dark rum. Stewart's, made here.
Well, not made here. Not even bottled,
actually. But they like it here, so the
company is owned here. Sort of. If you see
what I mean.

Sugary sweet. They drink it with Coke. I
don't. I like the treacley burn. Sweet
enough, that's me. Reminds me of Happymeals
at McDonalds with you two, when you were

Billy and Jerry and smaller. Happymeals. If
I buy you a Happymeal, will you be happy?
Is it magic? Does it work? Can we go back
to those Happymeal days, please? Please
please please please please please?

Wind's getting up. Howling. Never heard a
wind howl before I came here. Cables
holding the caravan down. It's warm in
here. Warm and wet with condensation.
Everything's wet, every morning. Unless it
gets really cold, and then it freezes. Not
nice. Not nice.

I wish I was at home with you. Warm and
cosy and with your mum. No I don't. Scratch
that. Forget it. We loved each other. Now,
I'm angry. So angry. For what she did. For
what she said to you.

May have to sell the bike, boys, if I'm
going to continue to live. No more running.
Nowhere left to run to. Here I am. Here I
am...

THE COMEDIAN'S WIFE

It was because I slept with a comedian's wife…
Yeah, yeah, that's right. A joke. A bad one.
But wait for the punchline…

VICTOR Murchison took me out in his boat one evening in May so calm the sea was like mercury. It was hot, too. Bizarrely hot, like we'd been transplanted to the Mediterranean.

"You get that here," said Victor, in his Brummie accent. "Spring can be day after day of Caribbean weather, the summer just a mess of bloody rain and wind."

He had come up with the rest of the travelling workers – bears, they called them, aptly enough in Victor's case – who built the terminal, and stayed on, salting away profits from a host of dodgy deals involving smuggled Sullom Voe equipment and misappropriated diesel. All of which he was happy to admit, once he'd downed a few Newcastle Browns.

There was a case of the stuff in the bottom of the *Lindisfarne*, Vic's boat. "All this water makes a lad thirsty," he said, juggling the wheel, an opener and two bottles.

I relieved him of the beer, and let him point the Lindisfarne

61

seaward along Ronas Voe, the closest thing Shetland has to a fjord. The towering granite bulk of Ronas Hill reflected coppery red, in the seashimmer.

"Red mercury," I mumbled, the sweet viscous beer catching at my throat.

"Aye, that's that nuclear stuff, isn't it?" said Vic. "Had one of them Russians offering me a kilo or something a couple o' weeks ago in the Thule Bar." Russian factory trawlers sometimes come into Lerwick to load up with herring, and there is healthy trade in legal and illegal material between their crews and local people. In the Soviet days, hundreds of eastern bloc boats would cram Bressay Sound, I'd been told, and the going was good for anyone with an old Lada to sell or some Zorki cameras to buy. Now, the pickings were leaner and involved much more dangerous substances. And people. If you believed the stories.

"Did you buy it, then?"

Vic laughed. "Naw. Asked him if he could get me a coupla of those Kalashnikov rifles, though. Might come in handy for shooting bloody seals. Sell them to the salmon farmers."

Vic launched into a measured rant about how seals were breeding like rabbits, and ever since the stupid soppy environmentalists had got them protected, they had eaten fishermen out of house and supertrawler.

"Not to mention tearing those salmon farms to bits, and munching their way through the stock, cool as they like."

"I thought salmon farmers were allowed to shoot them, if they were definitely causing them to lose fish?"

"Ah, but it's too late by then, boy, you see? Anyway, that's where I thought automatic weapons could come in handy. Maybe take out a few of them bloody Greenpeace bastards too."

I said nothing. I had seen a beach littered with seal corpses earlier in the year, and it had been a horrible sight. The beasts had been shot repeatedly by someone who clearly enjoyed what they were doing.

Victor stopped the engine. We were near the entrance to the voe, with nothing but open sea between us and the Faroe Islands, and despite the almost supernaturally windless evening, a long, steady swell was coming in from the north now, like the ripple of the world's muscle. Vic opened two more bottles of Newcastle Brown.

"Might as well cast a line or two, see if there's anything biting," he said. "Bit early for anything serious, like mackerel. Might get a cod or two if we're lucky, way the tide is." Birds were floating around us, unconcerned at this silent object moving with the slow waves. I could see puffins, so much smaller than you expected from those parrot pictures in magazines, and what I now knew to be guillemots. Tysties. A curious grey seal popped his whiskered, cat-dog head out of the water to peer at us.

"Bastard," shouted Vic. "God, if only I had one of those Kalashnikovs with me now! It would be kissed with a loving seal, pal!"

I laughed, dutifully.

I watched Victor run a line over the stern, baited with what he called a flee, a nylon trace festooned with hooks and coloured feathers, and sipped my beer. I didn't really know Vic that well. Not at all, in fact. He was just someone who drank in the St Rognvald; we'd had a few games of bad pool. Perhaps he was a serial killer. Maybe he had taken me out here to use me as bait for the fishes. Scenes from *The Godfather* and the *Sopranos* popped into my head. Luco Brazzi, eat your heart out.

"Came here with the terminal," said Vic at length, having hauled in his line empty several times. "Made a few bob. You know we were on 800 quid a week in 1978, scaffolders and painters? More than that from drifting timber off the site and over to Gluss Ayre, then selling it on. But you know all that."

Vic glugged at his Newcastle Brown. "Came here, like you, lived in a caravan. Liked it. Wife liked it. Good game of darts every so often, the fishing. Trout in the lochs, best rough trout fishing in Britain. Don't tell anyone. Didn't leave."

There was a pause, interrupted only by the slow slap of water on the hull, and the uninterested chirp and shriek of birds who clearly knew that Vic was wasting his time fishing.

"So what's your excuse then, mate? John? John Smith. Unusual name. I don't mean to be rude, overly curious, nosy, like. But you know, people get a tad curious. Stands to reason, really. Small place like this."

And as we sat and rocked gently in the Lindisfarne, named for Vic's favourite band, I realised that this was a kind of selection interview for membership of the Grunnawick and Eshaness community. Maybe Vic hadn't even been openly asked to grill me about my past. Probably not. It would just have evolved over an evening at the pub when I wasn't there, and someone would have said something about there being a bit of a mystery about that lad in the van, what was he doing here anyway, with his big BMW motorbike and his expensive clothes? Was he on the run? Was he some sort of child molester? Should we be careful around him with the kids? We need to know. And Vic would have nodded into his pint.

Actually, if I'd said to Vic: "Look, I'm a serial killer, I raped and pillaged my way across Europe, but honest, I just want a quiet life from now on." I think he may have simply shrugged and said: "Well, each to his own." The thing in an exposed island community is to know. Then you can act accordingly. I had already heard dark whispers about shotgun and digger accidents which had conveniently dispatched human hazards to community life.

There was still a warmth in the evening, and the movement of the boat was too slight to make me feel sick. It was almost calm as the Serpentine, but with that sense of being balanced on the curve of the earth. Of feeling its liquid heartbeat. I took a mouthful of ale as Vic tugged gently, hopefully on his fishing lines. I reached inside the poacher's pocket of my Drizabone, pulled out the paper-wrapped half-bottle of Trawler Rum.

"Fancy a wee nip?" I said.

***   ***   ***

Beginnings are always endings, and the business with the comedian's wife was the end of everything and the beginning of... well. I had thought I was at the beginning of the end, my end. My final farewell. But as it turns out, I haven't the courage. And maybe a bit too much curiosity.

Her name was Mary and I met her, inevitably, though her husband, a sliver-thin Irishman with staring alcohol eyes and greenish skin. He was, obviously a comedian, a Perrier Award winner, back down in London from the Edinburgh Festival and heading for big time telly: Channel Four were negotiating over a series, the Comedy Channel were trying to outbid them. Everyone wanted to talk to Feargal Mahoney. Everyone wanted a dose of his silkily charming surrealist banter.

Except his wife.

She was sick of him. And after a fortnight of running interference for the bastard, so was I. I was... what was I? A self-employed public relations bodyguard, really, a downmarket Max Clifford, I sometimes described myself. Basically, I was a poacher turned gamekeeper, a former tabloid hack now up for hire to people who wanted to stop tabloid hacks turning them over. Or wished to reap the commercial benefits of the turning over process for their own purposes. And I did very nicely out of it, too.

Oh yes, if you were a minor league politician caught on camera in a clinch with with a stripper, I might be able to deflect some of the unwanted attention heading for you like a tonne of elephant dung. As a dung shoveller, I was competent. If you were the stripper concerned, I could package you up, secrete you away in nice country B&B, and sell you to TV and the News of the Screws. I had the contacts. I had the chutzpah. I had the moral indifference.

My name then was Timmy Farrow.

A management company called Comic Belief, the biggest name in the business, had hired me to try and keep some kind of lid on the more sordid stories about Feargal which , as his fame began to impinge on the national consciousness, were emanating from women all over the country. It was pay-off time for waitresses in comedy clubs from Burnley to Bournemouth. Easy stuff, for the most part. Even the one or two he'd knocked about a bit had never pressed charges – that morning after Irish charm – but it was only a matter of time before some journo picked up on what was rapidly emerging as a true comedic liability. On the Barrymore scale of self-inflicted career damage, I would have given Feargal six out of ten. Not bad for someone who was essentially just starting out.

Then Feargal's wife said she was leaving him. Which was fair enough, except for the fact that she was a dangerous combination: anything but stupid, and bent on vengeance for all the shit she'd been put through during his rise from rambling barfly to rambling star turn. I went to see her.

"I was a nurse," she said, stamping around a tiny Battersea flat, glugging back bad South African Cab Sauv determinedly. She was from Dorset, I thought, the bumpkin burr in her voice strengthening the more she drank. "I worked all kinds of godless

66

shifts, wiped nasty old men's bums, washed out bloody bedpans, just so he could follow his so-called dream of stardom. Of bloody course I knew about the women. But he always swore it was nothing but roadkill. That was the word he used. Roadkill."

She was worn but beautiful, translucent coastal skin, piercing blue eyes and shorn dark hair. Attractive, no question. I sipped my red wine.

"That's... a fairly callous kind of... terminology, Mary."

"Damn right. Fuck the sisterhood. That's what he did. I mean, you put up with a lot, don't you? You put up with a lot, because you're expected to. Your mum and dad expect you to. Yourself... expects to."

"Yes, I'm sure."

"God, they're going to go mental. Go absolutely mental when this hits the papers. Mum and Dad. But I've got to get something out of this mess. They always said..."

It was a way in.

"You know, you really don't want to upset your parents, Mary. Hurt like that can be devastating. Think of their neighbours, and what they'll say. What they'll think." She said nothing, just looked at me, swaying slightly, a pair of small red Doc Martens in her hand. Why was she holding those shoes? Why do I remember that? "And you know, Comic Belief could..."

But suddenly she had dropped the shoes with a dull thumping clatter and she was in my arms, all black linen, a fresh smell of antiseptic and something I thought was Chanel, hot tears pumping onto my cheek.

"Oh God, Oh Jesus...oh God, that bastard... " And words to that effect. I patted her back gingerly at first, but she had the kind of body which moved and flexed and flowed until there was no escaping its demands. When the kissing started, there was no way back. And down in the dark domestic recesses of my mind,

67

a little voice was saying... nice move Timmy. This is what you get paid for.

Of course, she told Feargal. That was almost the first thing Mary did, in fact, once I was dressed and out of there, feeling the usual adulterous melange of guilt and satisfaction, self-hatred and pride.

I met him two days later in the green room at an independent TV studio in Docklands, where a fairly reputable production company (they sent limos, not taxis) was piloting a chat show format with him as scathing-but-cookie, daft cuddly Irish host. He greeted me with an embrace. Not knowing that Mary had been in touch with him, and feeling an odd desire to see her again (not sex, not love, no way; pity, probably, I told myself) I was a touch disconcerted.

"Fantastic, Timmy, absolutely fuckin' fantastic. Get the bitch off my back, why don't you? Off my back and onto hers. That's what we want... " He let me go, stood back, laughing, and then contemplatively swung a right hook nurtured, no doubt, during drunken brawls in the backstreets of Dublin or Cork. A crap punch. An amateur's.

It caught me a glancing blow on the right cheek bone, the kind of crack which serves mainly to enrage. It did. All the niceties of public relations executivedom, client privilege and professionalism went out the window in a welter of school playground fury. And I had gone to a tough school.

I grabbed his Armani lapels and nutted him right on the bridge of his prominent, comedic nose. Which proceeded to explode. It was hard to believe there could be that much blood inside the snivelling cretin's circulatory system.

Lives hinge on such incidents. My life. Feargal's. Not Mary's, though. Hers was over by then.

Mary had swallowed a combination of librium , paracetemol and diazepam, calculated carefully – she was a nurse, after all

– to be irreversible and fatal. No-one found her until just after the butting incident. It seemed she'd taken the pills just after phoning Feargal to tell him about our little liaison. His reaction, probably along the lines of "maybe that'll get you out of my hair, you bitch", may have been a disappointment to her, I don't know.

Feargal's nose was so badly broken he couldn't speak, work or even appear in public for over a month. The pilot show, of course, didn't go ahead. And just to make matters perfect, a man called Toby Rogers, showbusiness hack for The Sun, *had witnessed the entire altercation. When the news of Mary's death broke, he put two and one together and got... three. Full pages in a row, that is. One a day. For three days.*

None of this went down well with my wife and children.

*** *** ***

"Married?" said Victor. "You're married?"

"Technically. Even then we'd been separated for, oh, 18 months."

"Age?"

"Pardon?"

"What age are they? Your kids?"

I was always vague on this, even vaguer on actual birthdates. Dorothy had always taken care of that sort of thing, and when we parted... when I'd left, I had sent presents on a haphazard basis to Jerry and Billy. Eventually Dorothy had told me they didn't have birthdays three times a year.

"Fifteen," I said. "That's Jerry, 15. Or thereabouts. And Billy's 12."

"You think."

"Yes, I think. Look, it's just hard to explain what happened, how you kind of... I don't know. Blank them off. No, not blank.

They… It's like a wound. You leave it, it gets infected; you pick at it, it never heals. Or you leave it and somehow, scar tissue forms over it. Maybe. Eventually.

"So that's what your kids are, then, eh? A big scab that gives you occasional twinges?"

"Yes… no." The dark rum was almost gone. How could I tell Victor that to get by, you had to let the scars form. And that at any moment, unexpectedly, they could rip apart, wider and sorer and bloodier than ever? Or was that just me? Other fathers managed better. Dealt with it. Continued in legal contact and visitation arrangements. Faced up to things. Didn't run. What was wrong with me?

Vic hauled in his line. It was beginning to get cold. The *simmer dim* was making the light clot into a creamy luminous glow. It would not get completely dark at all, just fade down to a kind of bright twilight.

"Let's head in," Vic said.

"I left them," I muttered, mostly to myself. "I left them, but it was for my own good. I mean for their own good."

Vic looked at me, his face shadowed in the strange northern light. He said nothing.

*** *** ***

Dorothy (no diminutive; she hated it when people called her Dot or Dorrie) and I had split up over sex. Me having it, pretty much like Feargal with other women. Maybe that was why I hated Feargal so much. He was like me. Ruthless, a bad psychopathic kid in a sexual toyshop.

We'd worked out the custody thing, we thought. Decently. No Child Support Agency. Bare minimum of lawyers. Just the one crippling bill. It's a kind of moral fine, isn't it, the fee of a "family" lawyer? Dorothy kept the children, I paid maintenance. She moved to Colchester to be near her mother. I saw the kids every fortnight. If I could. Well, monthly. Or so.

Truth to tell (and you want the truth, do you? Are you sure?) I didn't see them much. And I could say it was hard, it was the agony, too much to bear. And it was, too. But other dads made the effort, got over the pain, forced themselves to do that Mcdonalds weekly, bi-weekly thing, the movies, the football matches, the bloody Pizzaland buffets.

I began making excuses. Dorothy made it easy to do that, as she gradually realised she could probably, if she played her cards carefully, rid herself of me completely, take her boys out of my pernicious influence. All that sex and drugs and alcohol and stuff. The motorbike I'd taken to hammering about London on, partly to save money, partly as a statement of Defiant Groovy Youthfulness.

Because there was all that. Sex, alcohol and mild drug stuff. Cocaine was always around, but I preferred speed. Cheaper, simpler, more direct. Bad side effects, bad comedown, but none of that self-aggrandizing shit. Basically, It was the only way a man of my age could keep up, sometimes. Keep it up. And if that meant waking up with a sore, clenched jaw, or lying frenziedly sleepless, fearful of heart failure, hearing taxis in a rainy street as huge, rushing speedboats, or the whisper of trees as violent radio static, louder than hell…well. It had to be worth it.

Anyway. I hadn't seen Dorothy or the kids for a long time. Maybe a month. Maybe two. I'd been busy, doing my job, earning money. Drinking and fucking around. Not sleeping in my former council flat in always-up'n'coming Peckham Rye. Burned out on bad amphetamines and Red Stripe deep in South London, day after day.

To tell you the truth, the thing with Feargal had been a lucky break. If you see what I mean. The original deal. The job.

71

Something chucked my way by a girl at Comic Belief who felt sorry for me. A last chance.

Then Mary and the Great Head Butting Incident. The three consecutive days in *The Sun*. The motorbike ride out to Colchester early on Saturday morning, cold, icy, a fortnight before Christmas. Walking with the boys to McDonalds.

I can tell you what they said. But Dorothy said they'd been picked on at school because of the stories. Because of their dad.

"I'm changing their name," she said. I looked at her stupidly

"What? From Billy and Jerry? William and Gerald? You chose them, for God's sake. Gerald was your dad's name. What to?"

"From Farrow," she said. To my maiden name. Divorce, too."

Divorce. We'd shied away from it, never wanting to admit… the finality. Names. "Not Sidebottom, Dorothy. You married me to get away from that anal moniker. Don't throw even that relief away. You think they won't get picked on for being called Bottom?" But I was reeling from the hurt. My name. My boys.

"To hell with you, Timmy," she said, bursting into tears, But she didn't throw herself in my arms like Mary.

She howled her way upstairs. Billy and Jerry were in the little terraced house's dining room, big boy on the Playstation, smaller on PC. Grand Theft Auto and Worms. I picked up my helmet and prepared to leave, feeling suddenly as if a giant numbness, a terrible chill, was surrounding me, eating into me.

I pushed open the dining room door, looked at the two boys, their faces blued and flickering in the cathode rays from their respective screens.

"Boys… I …"

They turned and looked at me, with a terrible indifference in their eyes. Or blame. Or… fear and agony. All the things I was feeling. Selfish, selfish, selfish. Go away go away go away…

A Randy Newman song popped into my mind: One of his trademark character studies, ambiguous identification with half-bad losers: a father takes delight in telling his son he's leaving home, with the cloying, searingly self-centred chorus, *I just want you to hurt like I do... honest I do.*

Honest I do.

All right then.

I turned and went out to the bike and rode back to London.

The cold kept coming. Through my leathers and gloves and into the heart of me, the core. I didn't think, only reacted. It was like being a robot, an android. I did things without thinking. Saw a dodgy, half-criminal lettings agent of my acquaintance. Gave him rights over the flat for a year, in exchange for six grand in cash. Hell, it was Christmas.

The Porsche raised another eight grand, also in cash, from some Primrose Hill dot-com adolescent. I flogged the contents of the flat through Loot. Kept the bike, a BMW. Took what clothes I could cram into the panniers, went out to Colchester for Christmas. One last time. One last look. Walked. Said goodbye to the boys. Gave them cash for their prezzies. No cards. Headed north.

Christmas Day.

From the Watford Gap Services I phoned Dorothy.

"Where are you?" she said. "What about Christmas? The boys don't want to see you or speak to you, so don't come here.

"I'm sending you five thousand quid, Dorothy." I said. Then I disconnected the mobile and switched it off. Actually, I changed my mind and sent her £2500. I always was a cheapskate. I gave the boys £100 each for Christmas. Was that enough? Money. Always money. Thing is, I kept the maintenance going. Biting down into savings, such as they were, eventually, once the trash cash was gone. By then I was fairly certain I would keep myself alive. One way or the other.

It was a horrible day, that Yule, as I've now learned to call it. Deep and crisp and even it was not. It was blustery and cold and wet. But a BMW is built to take that kind of thing in its stride, and so I battered my way north, feeling the numbness increase, and spread, like I imagine CJD does, until there's only a spark of your old self left, thinking and doing and living. Reacting. I kept on the M1, switched west, then north to the M6, kept going. And going.

*** *** ***

"Laboured all night and caught nothing," said Vic, as we tied the *Lindisfarne* up at his berth in the Heylor Marina.

"Right," I said, The combination of sea air and alcohol had me feel strange, spacy.

We stood on the wooden slats of the floating pier, which flexed gently beneath our feet. I wondered what Vic would do now, or say, or tell the others in the bar when I wasn't there. What he would spread about the community, and whether this was the end of my relationship with him, with the little group of local people who had, if not welcomed me, absorbed me.

"I nearly topped meself once," said Vic. "After I got laid off at the terminal."

I gaped at him. "Really? I thought you'd left... with plenty of, well, other options."

Vic shoved his hands deep into his pockets. "Well. No. Yes. I had made a bit on the side, over the years. Done all right with this and that out of the stores that should have stayed there, know what I mean? I mean, they couldn't prove anything, and when they sacked me, it was trumped up stuff. It was." He glared at me.

"Yes," I said.

"Anyway. I wouldn't have believed it. Thought it'd be great, free time, mess around at the house, the pub, go fishing. Enough cash, no problem. And I just fell apart. Bloody fell apart like… like a bloody *girl*. Doctor said it was depression, gave me these pills. But I tell you, I stood on the edge of the cliffs at Eshaness one day with a bottle of Grouse, and as near as dammit, that were it."

"Yes," I said. We began to move towards Vic's old Transit van, hand-painted and immaculate. Streakless.

"Got over it though. As you do. Things to live for." He pulled open the driver's door, which was, as ever in Shetland unlocked. "No kids, me and the wife. Always wanted them. Always. Both of us. No luck, though. No luck. Tried everything." He looked at me with something in his eyes which might have been accusation. Loss. Envy. Not anger. I didn't think so. "But things to live for nevertheless. You know. Football. Fishing." He flicked a hand at the shadowy beauty of the *simmer dim*. At Shetland. "This."

"Yes," I said. "This."

GET YOUR MOTOR RUNNING

MOTORBIKES chill you to the bone, turn the blood turgid and thick and slow. Even in summer; and this was winter in England.

I rode all Christmas night, along the spine of the country, warming up and dozing briefly in almost-deserted service stations. Tired and befuddled catering staff gazed at me without curiosity, from dull and desperate eyes. Tinsel twinkled from ceilings, and tinny carols played electronically as I ate bad motorway food, my leather trousers sticking to the stained plastic seats.

"Merry Christmas," said an emaciated, acne-ridden counter girl at a Burger King somewhere near Manchester, in the early hours of Boxing Day. Or to be precise, what she said was "nextpleasemerrychristmascanitakeyourorder" just like she had been told to, no doubt by the local representative of holy burger culture.

"Not any more," I said. "That's it done." I meant that it was Boxing Day, that Christmas Day had slipped by in the darkness. But she looked at me with such an expression of hatred and disgust I felt like Scrooge. Crossed with the monster from Alien. It was as if I had personally had Christmas cancelled forever.

"Large fries and a coffee," I said quickly. "Sorry." I hoped she wouldn't spit in the chips.

On a dull Boxing Day lunchtime I checked into a Motor Inn south of Glasgow, just off the M74, in a place called Motherwell. The hotel, if you could call it that, squatted next to a tawdry looking fairground, next to a massive area of parkland and lakes which looked curiously blackened and seared, and slightly unreal. A leaflet at reception told me it was reclaimed, once an industrial wasteland of slag heaps and dead industry. Now, with the River Clyde re-routed, it was a water park. Pictures of canoeists and windsurfers swam before my tired eyes as I lay on the huge bed in my room. There was a TV, but I ignored it.

I slept dreamlessly for seven hours, waking, ravenous in semi-darkness, the glow of sodium lights yellow beyond the curtains. I ached. It might have been an idea to take the biking gear off before lying down.

After a hot shower and a dreadful, steroid-swollen steak at the Beefhouse Grill which adjoined the Motor Inn, I walked across the car park and into the park. Illuminated pathways ran through sparse woodland and down to the artificial lake, and my cramped knees needed exercise. The whole place smelled of exhaust fumes, diesel oil and tar, and the noise of trucks and cars from the nearby motorway was a continual background thrum and whoosh.

At the edge of the water, a notice warned against swimming: "Anyone drinking this water should immediately seek medical advice," it added helpfully.

"Flooded mineshafts," said a voice behind me. "Heavy metals. Pollution from sewage works further up the Clyde. Ideal place to capsize a canoe, eh?" The accent was Scottish, that wheedling unctuous industrial Scots, post Billy Connolly. Male. Old. "Strange place this, in winter, eh?"

"I've… never been here before." I turned round. He was very elderly indeed, huddled in a parka and accompanied by a small dog of indeterminate and probably unfortunate breed.

"What? First time. Bad time of year, if you're, eh, cruising. Not much action."

"Sorry?"

"No, I understand. Don't want to interrupt. Not that way myself, you understand. Just walk the dog around here all the time, like, and you know, I can point you to the favourite spots, if you like. Then I'll be on my way, Not one for watching, Not that way inclined."

"I don't have a clue what you're on about. What do you…"

"Now, don't take offence sir, just being helpful. After all, this is where men come from all over the country, don't they, to be with… other men. Gay, I don't like that word. Makes me think of happiness. Aye, even in cold weather, I've seen it. Not that I watch, like. No sir. Just got to get Wee Tyson here back from his stravaigin' in the bushes, sometimes. That's all."

I began walking back to the Motor Inn, leaving the man with his dog and his denied, protested hopes for voyeurism. It seemed I had stumbled by accident onto Southern Scotland's top spot for gay trysts. The Hampstead Heath of Caledonia. I chuckled, but it didn't come out right. My face felt frozen, stiff from the hundreds of miles of cold motorcycle wind and rain.

Sex. This is where it could lead you. To open air fumbling in a frozen Scottish park smelling of oil and exhaust. To a lonely night in a godless Motor Inn. To a motorbike trip to… somewhere else. Away.

***   ***   ***

Maybe I should have gone south, I pondered next morning as, full of bad bacon and worse hash browns, I followed the signs through Glasgow for Oban and the north west. But half a day's riding south from London and you hit the Channel, and then it's a question of Abroad. Where they speak different languages, use different money, need identification, even passports, despite all this European Union stuff. It was such a separation, that. I didn't have the emotional resources to cope with it. And anyway, the masochist in me yearned for the cold, the purifying power of hail, ice, snow and clean rain.

Dirty Glasgow sprawled, big and tattered and sporadically, unexpectedly beautiful. It seemed there was hardly any space between the outer edge of the city and the Highlands. Loch Lomond. A song floated into my head: you take the high road, I'll take the low road. I'll be in Scotland before you. Death. A song about death, somebody had said. Who sang it? Some tiny Scotsman in a kilt with bandy legs? Stewart. Rod Stewart? Billy Stewart?

Andy, that was it. Andy Stewart. God, the loch was beautiful, and immense. The sky cleared, and hills began to appear on the opposite bank, big, hummocky things, not like alps or Himalyalas. Dour lumps of grass heather and rock. For a second, a flash of sunlight lent a golden aura to the road in front of me.

I left the loch behind, and began to climb into a more rugged, austere landscape. Suddenly, a sprawl of frontier-town ugliness appeared, something called Tyndrum. Tin Drum. Shuttered tour bus hotels for the aged and dying had been thrown up by the side of the road. I filled the bike with petrol, and ate unexpectedly well in a cafeteria called the Green Wellie. Attached to it was a shop selling everything from the rubber footwear which gave the place its name to mountaineering equipment, newspapers, books, awful Highland knick-knacks like ceramic haggises, and food. To my astonishment I spotted catering packs of sun-dried tomatoes piled on the floor.

I bought some mint imperials, and automatically smiled at

the sales assistant. She was tall, blonde and tanned, with a ring through her nose. Amazingly, she smiled back.

"Good Christmas mate?" Australian.

"Just… glad to get it by with," I replied.

"Know the feeling," she nodded. "Roll on New Year, I say." New Year. Hell's teeth. And they made such a fuss of it up here. What did they call it? Hogmanay. I shivered at the thought.

"Cold on a bike, mate, this time of year."

"Yes, but if it's all you got, you have to put up with it." But she was already serving another customer.

If I'd felt chilled before, Glencoe made my marrow freeze. Nothing had prepared me for the overwhelming scale and oppressiveness of the place. Especially uncased, unprotected, on a motorbike. The road seemed an embarrassing imposition on such a vast exercise in geological grandeur. But there was something there beyond sheer size, more than just epic scenery. Dimly, memories of the story came to me: The massacre of the MacDonalds by the Campbells, who had been welcomed into the local folk's houses according to the traditions of Highland hospitality. It was a tale of betrayal, of evil at its worst: the kind which you welcome openly into your house, and then turns on you without remorse or quarter.

Homewrecker. Homewrecker. Homewrecker.

I didn't stop. As the glen ended and the sea appeared, narrow at Ballachulish, I followed the signs for Oban, heading west. There were islands, I thought, and maybe I could reach one before the hellish antics of a Scottish new year broke upon me. Find somewhere to hide. To huddle. I was beginning to realise that while the Easy Rider ever-on-the-road trip might be possible in America in summer, winter Britain was no place for any would be Peter Fondas or Dennis Hoppers.

Oban tumbled down a steep hill, which was crowned by a strange, round coliseum-like structure, towards an attractive harbour. Islands appeared almost yards from the pier, it seemed, with shadowy bulks further out. "Your Holiday Island Gateway" said a notice. Piraeus it wasn't. I parked on the seafront and went into a small, snug bar with a log fire crackling in a cast iron grate. I drank whisky and listened to men with bad haircuts talking a language I didn't understand. It was like the speaking in tongues I'd once heard at a black Baptist church in Brixton.

When they left, I ordered another whisky and asked the barman where the men were from.

"Mull," he said. "I hear that they're some of the last Gaelic speakers on the island. Full of English, the place. Too handy for its own good." And he gave me a hard look. " They come here, the English folk the Sassenachs, and they buy up everything, every decent house. Most of them stay in them for a fortnight a year or something. They pay far more than any local can afford. It's because of the English I have to live in a caravan. In this bloody weather. The council house waiting list is as long as your arm." He slid the whisky over to me.

"I'm English."

"I know," he said.

*** *** ***

The crossing to Mull took about two hours, and it was dark by the time the massive car ferry docked at Craignure, an uneasy scatter of a place which barely seemed to exist. I clanked over the ramps and onto the island, following the signs to Tobermory, which avalanched down a cliff, like a smaller version of Oban, only without that weird crown-like folly on top.

I booked into a waterfront inn called, for some reason, the MishNish, and sat down to a substantial steak and chips, with good Guinness, again in front of a cliché roaring log fire.

Another Guinness and I could feel the deep coldness in my bones beginning to ebb away. Maybe this was a place to hide, to survive into the New Year.

Or perhaps not survive.

I found myself feeling indifferent, either way. Maybe it was just a case of eating, drinking, not thinking. Live to ride, ride to live, those Harley poseurs loved to chant. Until some articulated lorry sideswiped them into oblivion. Live to eat. Live to drink. Live to get by. Maybe in a cold, clear climate, on an island, I might do that. Survive. Get by.

***   ***   ***

In the days before New Year, with the weather clear and unexpectedly mild, I explored Tobermory, with its odd mixture of retired home counties bourgeoisie, struggling bed and breakfast operators and retiring locals. I ate good seafood and was almost tempted into a frosty game of golf, a game of my extreme youth. Until I saw the course, a coronary on every brutally steep fairway.

I rode the narrow Mull roads. It turned out to be a massive island, varied in its beauty, from mountain to vast sea-loch, forest to peat bog. I trundled down to the southern tip of the island and gazed over the water at Iona, burial place of the Scottish kings. A place of pilgrimage, but not for me. I felt myself growing stronger, more at ease with myself. What was left, after cutting off the bit which used to have kids, a wife, a lover who died, a career. The bit with a life. The amputation scars were healing, I told myself.

On New Year's Eve, I found myself beneath the vast escarpment of Gribun, the huge line of soaring cliffs facing out onto Loch na Keal. The road was like the one in Glencoe, tiny beneath the huge cliffs, making you flinch as you rode along it. Except here there was the sea on the other side.

An island, oddly shaped, flat and with a sandy beach, hunkered down just a hundred metres or so offshore. A curiously shaped building, square and slab-like protruded from its surface like a blockhouse or bunker. I stopped the bike and walked across the rocky beach until I was as near as I could get. The building was a kind of concrete castle, obviously a large dwelling house, but strange and sinister, angular and inappropriate. Horribly out of place, as if dropped by masonic aliens with a fetish for cement. There were no fences around it, and as far as I could see, no gardens.

As I walked back to the bike, I noticed that a small, black swastika had been painted neatly on the back of the litter bin next to the lay-by. The kind of graffiti you might see anywhere, yet it gave me an odd, queasy feeling. It had been painted with care, and recently, not by some daft, time-warped punk. As I got closer, I saw that someone had left a small bunch of flowers, small white blooms I didn't recognise, at the bottom of the bin, pinned down by a stone. They were wilting now, but they couldn't have been more than a few days old.

I felt my skin crawling, and nervously looked up and down the narrow seaside road. But there was no-one.

*** *** ***

They had been good to me in the MishNish. Friendly and open, the staff were a mixture of Scots and English, and they were used to strangers blowing in for brief periods of shelter.

"Yachties, mostly, in the season, John," said Frankie, a local girl whose husband, Keith, had a lobster boat. "Get all kinds in here, all nationalities. French, Swedish, German…"

"Talking of German, I said, there was something…"

83

"Talk to you in a minute, John," she said. "Got to change a barrel."

I was already John Smith. He was the survivor. John Smith. A cipher. A nothing. Late leader of the Labour Party. But he was dead. He was dead too.

The place was getting busy. There were a fair few guests staying for the delights of an island Hogmanay, and I had been cordial enough in saying hallo to them over breakfast or a pint, without wanting to get too close, or sway too much. Tonight, the bar would stay open into the small hours, and doubtless there would be much kissing and hugging around midnight. I decided not be around for that.

So at around 11, with the place heaving, I struggled through the throng to the door, a half-bottle of Oban single malt and a tin of Carlsberg Special in my pockets, and felt with relief the pure, cold, salty air hit my face. I walked up the steep switchback behind the Mish Nish and followed the road until it ran out of light, up on to the golf course behind the town, that impossibly perpendicular. You could get vertigo playing an iron shot.

And there I drank the half bottle down, neat, gulp after gulp, feeling the hot spirit in my throat and gut, and all the time rattling the box of DF118s I'd had with me ever since leaving London. A present from a casual pharmacist friend. Or thief and dope dealer if you prefer.

I sat on the edge of a bunker as I contemplated swallowing them on top of the whisky, washed down with Danish beer. What would happen? I'd sleep. Possibly vomit and choke to death, Hendrix style. Certainly freeze. The temperature was dropping and a frosty haze was forming over the lights below. I could hear church bells ringing, and the distant sound of music and shouting.

Ugly. It would be ugly. How about the kids? What would

they think? But no, that part of me was gone. Cut away, lost. Same for Dorothy. It would be punishment for her, though. But did she deserve that? Yes. Oh yes.

No.

Actually, If I stayed long enough on the golf course, I wouldn't need the pills. The drink would be enough. I could feel a deep lethargy overtaking me. And then I was up, moving, walking, stumbling, drunk as a skunk, but colder. I could survive, I told myself. I would. Not feeling, not thinking. Just surviving. I could do that. Maybe here, on this island. I would start the new year as an islander. Learning to live.

On the road up from the harbourfront, small groups of swaying and singing people greeted me. I didn't recognise any of them. "Happy New Year," they cried. A woman kissed me wetly. I could feel the spittle freezing on my chin.

The Mish Nish was still busy, and a few musicians were drunkenly strumming and bowing jigs and reels in a corner. But the crowd had thinned out, with household celebrations and parties calling the loyal home to their loved and hated ones. I slumped onto a stool.

"One for the road, *mo graidh*?" It was Frankie. She leaned over and kissed my forehead. "A good new year to you, Johnny."

"Mo… mo gray?"

"My darling, my darling… it's Gaelic. Mind you, I have a darling at home, John. Johnny It's term of endearment, you might say.

"Casual. You always so… casual?" She laughed.

"Och, anyone would think you'd been drinking, John. But listen, weren't you going to ask me something, earlier? I don't drink, you see. I remember things. It's what I'm good at."

But I couldn't remember. My brain felt like a coracle in a storm. I tried to think.

"Down on at Loch na Keal today… can't remember… an island. Funny house."

Frankie smiled. "Inchkenneth. Ah yes, Iona's granary they used to say, once run by nuns. A lovely place."

"Flowers… there were…"

"Aye, in the spring it's lovely for wild flowers. Carpeted with them. They say that's what Unity loved most about it.

"Unity?"

"Och, you don't know about Unity? People come from all over to see the place where Unity lived and died. She's become a bit of a saint. In a manner of speaking. Not everybody approves."

I gazed at Frankie. My lips felt disconnected, puffy. I tried to speak; failed.

"Unity Mitford. Hitler's mistress." She was speaking as if to a dull child. "You know, one of the famous Mitford sisters. Went to Germany, fell in love with the whole Nazi thing. Watched Jews eat grass, or so they say. Shot herself in Germany when she realised Britain was going to fight her beloved fuhrer. She didn't die, though. The bullet lodged in her brain. The family put her away. Here. Or on Inchkenneth, rather. Like a prisoner. They say she used to roam the island at night signalling for a U-boat to come and pick her her up. Mad as a brush, poor dear. Probably was even before she shot herself. Died after the war. She was still here. I know a man who danced with her once. And now they come to sniff around at her memory. Still, that's tourism, isn't it? Do you want a wee dram now, darling?"

I shook my head. A bad mistake. The room twirled and heaved. So did I. I ran, tripping and falling for the door. I could hear Frankie's laughter in the background. No hope with her. No hope anyway, she was married. I reached the railing at the sea wall, and managed to be sick into someone's moored creel boat. I hoped it was Frankie's husband's. How dare she be married? Bitch.

The cold air, revived me a little, though. And I thought of that painstakingly-painted swastika on the waste bin near Inchkenneth. And the bunch of white, jewel-like flowers. I stood up, my throat burning. Shakily I turned to walk back towards the MishNish.

Edelweiss, I thought. The flowers were edelweiss.

Suddenly I felt sick again.

*** *** ***

Nothing moved on Mull on the 1st of January. Certainly not me. At least not until the evening, when I managed to down two quick pints of Extra Cold Guinness and a disgusting microwaved mince pie. Next morning, the second, the ferries started running again. Hopefully with the captain and crew fully recovered from their traditional Scottish celebrations.

There was no sign of Frankie when I left. Her boss, a New Zealander called Mick – I was beginning to wonder how the Scottish tourism industry survived without antipodeans – made up my bill and swiped my credit card.

"Thought your name was John," he said, as I signed the slip. "John Smith. Memorable name."

"It is," I shrugged. "But only for sexual purposes." He smiled.

"Good luck, then. Johnny."

The big Caledonian MacBrayne ship wallowed in an uneasy sea. I kept on deck, letting the wind wipe the sourness out of my head. I looked back at Mull, at its massive beauty, and wondered about the swastika, the white flowers. I had thought nothing about it until Frankie had told me that story. Unity Mitford. Waiting in the dark night of a damaged brain, year after year for the submarine her Nazi god-lover never sent. Maybe it was crap.

Maybe it was just a tale for Nazi-chic holidaymakers. But deep down I knew it was true. And there was a sickness there that was forever going to stain Mull for me.

Christ, I thought, you come so far, you come to this edge of Europe, and you find the spores of the continent's darkest evil, just lying by the side of the roads. Disguised as flowers.

There was more to Britain than this. There was more to Scotland. There was more of the landmass to go, more to the north. I rolled off the ferry and took the Fort William road.

*** *** ***

For a week I explored single track byways in the north west, as the weather worsened. I took shelter in a tiny hotel near Durness, in Sutherland, for two days until the icy winds moderated into slower-moving grey murk. Fortunately there was no snow. Loch Eriboll, with its strange quarry workings and military remnants, reminded me of Mull. Caithness seemed utterly dominated by the sinister dome of the Dounreay nuclear plant. I caught the ferry for the short but unbelievably rough crossing to Orkney, and thought I'd found the place I wanted. The light, in the brief blink of day you got at that time of year. The treeless, stark bigness of the skies. The low horizons. But one visit to the Italian Chapel on Holm, across the Churchill Barriers, was enough. There was death here too, death and evil represented by the massive concrete blocks, the sunken ships and the chapel itself, commemorating the thousands of Italian Prisoners of war who had been used by the British as slave labour here, to build the massive causeways.

Many died. And they were there because over 800 men had drowned when a German submarine sank the battleship Royal Oak in Scapa Flow, early in the Second World War. Scapa Flow, which also held the wrecks of the First World War German

Grand Fleet. Where divers died each year trying to steal lumps off the giant hulks. Everything smelt of death.

I suppose I knew it was me that smelt of death really, that I was sniffing at my own suppuration. Sensing my own decay. But you can fool yourself on a motorbike. Keep moving, keep going, and you'll find what you're looking for. Whatever that is. Clean air. Fast air.

But where else was there to go?

In the tiny public bar of the Stromness Hotel, called The Flattie, I was drinking dark rum, mainly because it was there, and it felt right to be drinking something called Trawler Rum, deep and warm and Caribbean in such a cold and northerly spot. It was a Saturday night, eight or thereabouts, and the place was crowded, but I wasn't giving up my barstool for anyone.

The man next to me was English, a diver on the piss.

"Up for a week's piddling about on the Royal Oak, see what we can filch," he muttered in a Yorkshire accent. "Dunno where the rest of them are. Been at it since we got off the boat this morning. Back down tomorrow."

"Isn't it…"

"Illegal? Yeah. War grave all that. Nothing left, though not really. All gone. Too many been there already, you see. Still, you have to try."

"Actually, I meant… dangerous. Aren't you risking… aren't you taking a chance, what with all the drink still in your system?"

He gazed deep into his pint of Caffreys.

"Nah. Nitrogen. Nitrogen's what they use to put the bubbles in this stuff. That's what you need. Nitrogen."

"I thought nitrogen actually gave you the bends…"

"Yeah, well. I'm the fucking diver, pal. This is my nitrogen, and if I want to use it, I will. Nitrogen. Nitrogen is good for you."

Just then a huge, groaning howling noise shook the bottles on the gantry behind the bar, and made the hairs on the back of my neck twitch.

"What the hell…"

The diver hadn't moved. "Hjaltland, that's what that is, pal. The Shetland boat. There's more of these bloody islands, you know, eight hours up towards the North Pole."

I finished my pint and walked outside. The harbour's skyline was now dominated by a blue and white ship bearing the two words North and Link on its side, capitalized and run together: NorthLink. The boat was manoeuvring itself gently into dock, backwards.

I walked to the PO ticket office, and booked the bike and myself on for the next morning's eight-hour trip to Lerwick in the Shetland Isles. The girl at the counter was friendly, thoroughly Orcadian with her sing-song, almost Welsh voice.

"Where've you come from sir?"

"London."

"On a motorbike, at this time of year? You must be hardy." And she giggled. "Bound for Shetland. Well that's it. The end. The edge of the world, the Romans called it."

"Is that right?"

"Yes. Thule. Ultima Thule. Once you're there, there's nowhere else to get to before the Faroe islands, or Iceland. And then the North Pole. It's the last of Britain. Big winds. Bigger than here. Blow you off your feet. And bare. They don't have cows there, you know. They just fly off the edge. It's the island of the lost, the say. Islands." She laughed, showing she was only joking. I wondered how long Orcadians had been saying that about their northern neighbours. "Can I have your name, sir?"

"Smith," I said. "John… Smith."

This time I paid in cash.

Hi Billy
Hi Jerry

Just wanted to say... I'm missing you.
Thinking about you. Wondering how you are.

I'm sitting outside, outside at 11
o'clock at night, and it's light. Still
light, and still, very still.

I wish you could see it. Both of you.
Though I know you'd be bored. Wondering if
you could get a Burger King. Wishing for a
Gamecube or a souped up PC. And all I've
got is an old, rusty Olympia typewriter
Dodie Two Hats gave me.

Dodie Two Hats. I wonder what you'd make
of him. He's funny. A character.

I could take you out on a boat. Get
Victor to take us fishing. We could motor
or row, set some lines and just drift,
drift out of Ronas Voe to the open sea,
where nothing, not the quietest, most
windless night, stops the breakers from
giving you the willies. Well, me. I'm
easily frightened.

They call this the simmer dim. The
midnight sun. So far north. In the winter,
when I first got here, I sometimes saw the
aurora, the Northern lights. Da Merry
Dancers, they say hereabouts.

It's a good place. It's where people
come, where people like me end up. Island
of lost souls. Lost fathers.

Look, what I wanted to say was... I don't

know. That it's only begun to strike me how much I might have devalued you. Taken away your sense of your own worth. Made you feel this was somehow your fault.

No, no no. I was going to say it's me, I'm the worthless one. But maybe in a way that makes it worse for you. Sons of a worthless father.

How can I make you feel valued, feel special and good and happy? Not by coming back. No, not that. I can't anyway. I couldn't.

I know your mother loves you, and works to make you whole and healed and to give you... a good life. But the joy, the joy that should be there...is it? Is it joyful for you. Did I break the joy out of you and throw it away? Do you feel joy? Do you feel anything?

I stopped feeling. I can remember a time when I felt things — when I felt love and joy and calmness and happiness. I can remember being your age, and the vast, overwhelming excitement of simple things. A bike. That great wind-roaring eruption of speed, coming down a hill, freewheeling, never being out of breath, never feeling unfit. Or that's how it seems now. First time my dad took me to see a football match, hoping I would end up, like him, an eternal West Ham supporter. And how I loved the crowd, and the being there, being with him. Even if the football thing never stuck with me.

Maybe I should have done that with you, taken you to more football matches. Remember when I got you tickets for Arsenal v Man U? Got freebies from a friend who used to be Robbie Fowler's agent, still had connections? How was I to know you were both Chelsea supporters by then? You should have said, lads.

I should have asked.

Maybe the best thing I can do is stay away. Let the wounds heal. Let the joy begin again, without me. Maybe that's your best bet.

Still, I wish you could see this. I really do. Maybe it's sentimental shit, but I wish we could sit here and look out at the sea, at the tirricks whirling and chittering, and talk about things. Or play cards.

Or just...

Never mind.

Never mind.

What I want to say is that I wish you all the best. No, that sounds so stiff and stupid. I want the best for you. At first I thought that the best would include me being permanently out of the picture. For keeps. For good. But who knows what coping with that would do to you? Or is that being selfish too; overestimating my own worth?

I do, though. Wish you all that's good.

The very best of everything. Can I help
repair things? Can I?
   I don't know.
   Lots of love, and say hallo to your
mother for me.

   Dad

PUBLIC RELATIONS

I COULD feel Christmas looming, threatening, like doom, from the beginning of December. It was in the shops, with the sprouting of tinsel and fake holly. The TV in the St Rognvald's bar seemed eternally populated by Santas selling toytown tat. Hopes were high in Northmavine that we would have our very own tawdry, moneyspinning Santaland, someday soon. We would all be elves. And far away, in London, the boys waited for the outpouring of love and generosity and hope and joy that the 25th of December is meant to bring.

Or maybe they didn't. I hadn't spoken to them since that cold day of departure. In the past they had always been filled with that huge festive excitement, the expectation that come Christmas, everything would change, all would be well.

We had shared that hope, against all odds, year after deteriorating year, as the marriage fell into disrepair, became irreperable. Still, we would clean up the house for Christmas, shuffle the furniture, decorate, dress the tattered, shabby halls with boughs of plastic holly. Come the day, we would luxuriate in a warm glow of children's enjoyment and alcohol. Until the drink began to wear off and the viciousness started with the hangovers.

*** *** ***

Darkness. I'd never known such darkness. Days blinked briefly, sometimes bathed in a low golden glow, sometimes never coming to life at all, huddling in a blue, restless twilight torn and battered by colossal winds carrying rain, sleet and despair. Frosts clamped the calm days with a fearsome grip which could freeze peat stacks so hard you had to use a pick to get your few scraps of burning out. The sea would jangle and crackle as it froze like cheap vodka into a mixture of spiky shards and brown mush. Wind chill was positively dangerous. I bought a huge padded canvas parka from North Eastern Farmers, and one of those IRA balaclavas with the sinister stitched eyeholes. I would huddle at my little iron stove as the wind howled and shrieked outside.

Sometimes I would struggle out, through the good weather, or bad, to the phone box at the turn-off, and attempt to dial a number. There was no telephone at the house. I hadn't even attempted to have on installed, and thought the cost would probably be vast, anyway. I had heard of some poor soul in an isolated cottage who had been charged £20,000 for the installation of a line.

Anyway, phonebox-bound, with the sound of sheep and wind all around, I could never complete the call. Once, I heard her voice, but I put the phone down without saying anything.

And that was a mistake. Isolation had made me careless. Or it could have been the three large rums in the St Rognvald beforehand. As I headed back along the rain-hammered road to Scraada, I could hear the sound of a phone ringing, and realised she had dialled 1471. With a few enquiries, she would know where I was.

And maybe that's what I'd wanted all along.

*** *** ***

"Ever thought of maybe getting a job?"

It was Alastair Wyllie speaking, sitting next to me at the St Rognvald bar while some dimwitted children's entertainer hyperventilated on the TV above us about a new Playstation game called something like Nuke the White House. I had a cold, just to make me even more snottily miserable than usual, and was drinking whisky macs – cheap whisky and Crabbies green ginger wine. It was the ultimate hangover drink. Giving, not soothing.

"A job?" The thought was a novel one. Since my arrival, no-one had seemed surprised that I possessed no visible means of support, that I could run a motorcycle and spend money on sometimes indulgent drinking without actually doing anything to obtain monetary reward. But the fact that I'd had to sell the bike had not gone unnoticed. Nothing did.

"Aye. Maybe you're needing a bit of extra cash, what with Christmas and everything?"

I thought about the BMW. My mobile mid-life crisis Dorothy had called it, way back in the days when I was a married man allowed such innocent distractions. Nothing special, not one of those Kensington Harleys, ridden by the moneyed dreamers of some English-American dream. Just a well-looked-after R100 which could support even a thinly-padded bottom for several hundred miles per day. It had brought me here, and through wind, rain sun and hail taken me around the islands, in and out to Lerwick, on wobbly trips to and from the pub. Then the money had begun to run out.

"I don't know, Alastair. What sort of a job?" Alastair ran a smokehouse and fish processing plant halfway down the road south to Brae. Mid-Shetland Seafoods, it was called. They

97

advertised for filleters and gutters and labourers regularly, and the rates seemed reasonable. But my fish gutting and filleting experience was limited to fumbled slicing at presents left at the caravan door since my arrival in Shetland. I didn't know my megrims from my black scabbards.

"Public relations," said Alastair. "Need to sort out our marketing. Got a wee, eh, marketing problem. And a bit of help on the kippering line wouldn't go amiss. Maybe some lifting. Your back's all right, isn't it?

I was stunned. Who had I told about my past life as that loathsome creature, the professional PR person? Nobody, as far as I could remember. Not unless I had babbled something when soaked in rum, but even then…

"What makes you think I would know anything about PR, Alastair?"

"Ach, you've got one of those nice English accents, John, and you seem to be able to talk without slurring your words too much." Alastair swept the hank of grey hair from his round, florid face. "That seems to be what a public relations person needs. It's not exactly skilled, work, is it? I mean, not like filleting. How does six quid an hour sound? You can get a lift to the factory with me." He finished the dregs of his pint. "And I was joking about the kippering. And the lifting."

I thought about the idea of abandoning my closeted winter life of reading library books, going for solitary, swaying walks. Seeing Alf, Victor, Mel and the others at the St Rognvald, and eking out what little drink money remained. And then I thought: Christmas. Presents for the boys. I'll need to do something.

"Are you sure you haven't been… this PR thing…"

"What?"

"Well, maybe I do know something about it. That side of things. I can't believe you were just guessing, Alastair. or thought my accent was appealing."

He sipped thoughtfully at his pint.

"Somebody phoned the hotel the other lunchtime, asking for a... for a Mister Barrow... or Farrow. Some woman. Wouldn't believe Mel when she said no-one by that name lived around here, as darling Melissa would. Anyway, this woman said you were in public relations, that you looked like a public relations man. Couldn't be mistaken for anything else. Didn't Mel tell you?"

We both looked at the redoubtable Mel, all bleached blonde number two and broken veins, who was busily polishing glasses. She had been preoccupied for weeks, no doubt thinking about her baby son. She lived alone with the two-year-old, who didn't keep well. Nobody knew who, or where, the father was.

She shrugged. "Don't know any Barrow," she mumbled, "or Farrow. Narrow. Harrow. What kind of name is that?"

My name is John Smith. I keep telling myself that. Smith, Smith, Smith. "A bad one," I said. "No-one here by that moniker. Quite right, Mel. Didn't say who she was? The woman phoning?"

But neither Alastair nor Mel had to say. I already knew.

So it was that in the blackness of a frostbitten December Monday morning, I found myself out of bed and enveloped in the warmth of a Vauxhall Senator, listening to Radio Two as Alastair told me about his "little marketing problem."

"It's like this, John. There's this product we've got. Salmon fillets. And, what can I say? Something seems to have happened to the... well. They come blast-frozen in little sealed plastic containers, and... " He fell silent, shaking his head as the sound of Terry Wogan chortling permeated the hot interior of the car. "I'll need to show you."

We parked behind the large steel shed which housed Mid-Shetland Seafoods, and Alastair switched off the engine. He made no move to get out.

"You can be discreet, John, can't you? I thought you were the man for this, because you seem to be that. Discreet."

Curious, but confused, I nodded. "And you're an open minded sort of fellow, I expect. But sensible. Not gullible." I nodded again. With a grimace, he opened the door, allowing a blast of refrigerated air into the car. It was time to go to work.

Everyone inside the factory was dressed in white from ridiculous pork pie hats for the men and odd, semi-medical net things for the women to the tips of the ubiquitous white Wellington boots. Soon I was monochrome too. It felt weird, like dressing up as a ghost at Halloween. Only smellier. The reek of fish was everywhere. It's funny how fish is just a generic perfume. You don't get a difference between mackerel or haddock or crab sticks. It's just fish. And Mid-Shetland Seafoods was fishiness central.

I was shown the kipper line, the salmon filleting tables, the smoking ovens, the whitefish area, and the packing section. It was among the most boring experiences of my life, but of a type I was familiar with from my years in PR. You had to do it. The client, who generally was enthusiastic, probably obsessive, sometimes psychotic about whatever they produced, be it lawnmowers or pornography, would insist on showing you the tedious nuts and bolts of production, and you would nod and grin and half-listen, looking for the story, the tag, the hook. This is Brenda, someone would say, she's just out of prison for attempted murder. Hmm, Might make something of that, you would think. Get the company's name in *The Sun*, how does that sound? This is a knife factory after all. Any chance she used one of your blades? The tabloids might be interested…

But though there were knives aplenty at Mid-Shetland Seafoods, it was a fish factory. And after a while, even Alastair appeared to realise that there was only so much seafood a man could take.

Finally we repaired to the clutch of interlinked Portacabins which made up the offices. I removed my stupid ghost hat and took the coffee his secretary, a nose-ringed goth called Alison, offered me.

"Alastair," I began. "I really don't think…"

"It's Madonna," he blurted suddenly. "Madonna and child. I know you don't really have any interest in kippering or whatever, John, but if you could help with this Madonna thing, I'd be grateful. I mean, it's getting completely out of hand."

Visions of Guy Ritchie, Ms Ciccone, pointy steel-tipped breasts and that book of sex photographs she produced swirled around my mind. And child? What had she called her offspring? Rocco? Rocky?

"Are you… I mean, I didn't think Madonna advertised anyone's products, Alastair. How did you manage to get her on board? Must be some sort of joint seafood marketing initiative, right? Like a virgin, Shetland shellfish is pure and unsullied… but isn't she a vegetarian?"

Alastair looked steadily at me.

"Not Madonna. THE Madonna. The Virgin Mary. And Jesus, not Rocky. Jesus Christ, am I not making myself clear?" Alastair suddenly stood up and walked over to a large industrial fridge. He took something out, then dumped it on the table in front of me. "Take a look."

Out of a white plastic bag I carefully pulled one of the frozen ready meals Mid-Shetland Seafoods produced. It had defrosted and felt slightly slimy. The colour cardboard sleeve had a fairly appetising picture of a salmon steak, delicately pink and covered in a fluorescent green sauce. "Fresh Shetland Salmon Fiorucci in Persto Sauce," some gothic letter said.

"Alastair," I began, "surely it's 'pesto sauce', not 'persto'?"

"Shetland dialect word. You wouldn't understand. Open it."

I slipped the sealed plastic tub from its covering and gazed at the opaque cellophane surface. Nothing leapt out at me, such as an infestation of killer posion arrow frogs or verminous sea worms. Gingerly, I pulled the tab at one corner. It was loose. The fragrance of fish and something pungent, possibly rancid pesto, hit me full in the face as I tugged it back.

"Christ," I said.

"Quite," replied Alastair. "And His Mother. But not on a bike."

The salmon steak, round and pink, pay in a bed of green sauce. And in the flakey filligree layers of the salmon's flesh, an image of the Madonna and her baby son was clearly visible. This was no Turin Shroud. This was unmistakeable. Like a stamp.

"It's like a computer graphic onto that piece of fish," I said. "Bloody hell, how many like this are there?"

"So far, about a dozen have turned up," said Alastair. "This one was clocked at a wholesaler's in London, when some light-fingered clerk fancied a snack. It appeared half way through the microwaving. But here's the thing: it's from a consignment that was about to go to Cuba, where unless I'm much mistaken in my admittedly dim appreciation of Marxist theory, they're not too keen on divine apparitions and miracles. I don't think Fidel would like it."

"What about the rest?"

"Well, we opened everything we had in stock, resealed the… unholy ones. A dozen. But there's bound to be more already out there. Persto Fiorucci is one of our best lines, though it was slipping a bit … Anyway, that's why you're here."

"What… what do you want me to do?"

"Well, basically just sit here and wait for somebody in, say, Mexico to phone up and say that Jesus and his mum have been revealed in a piece of Shetland salmon in pesto… I mean persto… sauce. That the fish distributor's warehouse has been

102

besieged by 10,000 screaming pilgrims. That they're raising money to build a refrigerated chapel. That we're being sued by the relatives of the 100 people so far trampled to death." Alastair was a dark purple colour. A vein throbbed in his temple. Involuntarily I jerked back in case I was spattered with gore when a blood vessel exploded.

I slumped in my chair, heavily. From having escaped the rat race of public relations in London, I was now sitting in a fish factory in the Shetland Islands in winter, facing quite the most bizarre PR crisis of my career. And on a worldwide, indeed almighty scale.

"How many countries do you send fish to, Alastair?"

"I don't know. Och, yes I do. Maybe 15."

"And who do you think is doing this? Apart from the obvious suspect of course."

"No, it's not God. I've had our food scientists check out the affected fish, and it's being done with food colouring. It's safe enough. Exactly how they're getting so exact an image I don't know. Maybe gelatine printing. Like with jelly? Works a treat, or so I believe. But it's somebody here, and I'm going to find out who."

"Just find out who's religious. I mean Roman Catholics, presumably… "

"Well, you're not allowed to ask that kind of question any more, even if you wanted to, which I don't," said Alastair, who was now turning as pink as one of his salmon portions, though without the green sauce. "Someone's faith is their own business. And anyway, there are no Roman Catholics here. I'd know, wouldn't I? This is hardly Dublin's fair city, is it? This is somebody's idea of a joke, and by God… " he thumped the desk, and the blessed salmon portion jumped from it s bed of green as if possessed with the spirit of a live fish, "I'm going to to find out who."

"Before you fly off the handle, Alastair, have you looked at the positive aspects of this? I mean, with Christmas coming up and everything, this could be a whole new dimension in festive marketing." I heard myself speaking, but I couldn't believe the old crap was still in there. Yet out it came. "Can't you hear it? 'At the time of advent, eat the Christian symbol of the fish, and if you're lucky, blessed, whatever, you too might actually find Jesus and Mary in your dinner… ' It's a bit like one of those win-a-car offers, isn't it? 'Is there a magic winning card in your packet of crisps? Win a blender!' Only more, well. Seasonal."

Alastair looked at me, shaking his head slowly. "Jesus Christ," he said. "How long have you been out of public relations?"

Not long enough, I wanted to say. But then a phone on Alastair's desk, one of three, rang with a particularly shrill note. He picked up the receiver, listened for a moment, then put it down without speaking.

"One of them has turned up," he muttered.

"Where?"

"In a Jewish lunch club in north London. You can imagine how amused they are. They're talking about cancelling their order. Some poor old widow was just about to tuck into her salmon steak al la persto Fiorucci, and what does she see? Not Rabbi Lionel Blue, I can assure you."

I sighed. "I'll need a phone and a computer," I said. "Internet access. All that stuff." I could feel something stirring within me. It felt oddly like indigestion. Or excitement.

*** *** ***

Two days later, the first journalists were booked on a plane from Heathrow (via countless stops in places like Wick) after what *The Sun* was calling A Madonna Meal and the *Star* a Holy

Smoked (despite the fact that the fish was fresh, or fresh frozen) had sparked an outbreak of spiritual fervour in Seville and the sealing off of a fridge in the kitchen of a church belonging to a charismatic Christadelphian sect in Brixton. There were queues stretching half a mile just to peer in the freezer compartment of this old Frigidaire, though the minister, a Ghanaian who laboured under the name Nelson Mandela Hitler, had convinced his local branch of Comet to provide an extra-large American-style upright freezer with a glass door to provide a new home for the salmon up near his pulpit.

I had issued a statement as soon as the first professionally bored newsdesk calls started coming in, basically, as Alastair had forcefully instructed me, playing down the whole thing as "a workforce prank", and pointing out that tests on the images found so far had proved beyond doubt that the Madonna and child were not naturally occurring, but comprised what looked like a stencilled or transferred shape in cochineal food colouring.

"This won't work," I told Alastair. "Does the expression 'never let the facts get in the way of a good story' mean anything to you?" He just frowned, pursed his lips and turned away.

I was getting used to the concept of working for a living again. Out of bed in the darkness, quick cup of tea, out to meet Alastair, then by comfy car through a tunnel of darkness, into the brilliant fluorescence of the factory office. I got to know the secretaries, Alice and Mandy, and the salesmen, Rob, Eric and Victor. And as the pressure grew, and the story spread, onto the local radio station and newspaper, *The Shetland Times,* the workforce became infected with excitement of it all.

"What's du think, then, Johnny?" asked a filleter one day, grabbing a fag outside, still dressed in his white angelic wellies, coat and strange trilby. "Is God playing tricks on us?"

Rob, one of the salesmen, was also grabbing a quick Silk

Cut. "Aye, well," he said, "God knows the orders are enormous. We can't keep up. Can't get the supplies."

I said nothing. I had journalists to prepare for. Phil Janes from *The Sun* and Val Riddock from *The Guardian*. News hacks. I'd dealt with neither of them before, in my previous life, and there was a chance they wouldn't recognise me when we met. Wouldn't remember those three days in *The Sun*. Feargal and Mary and me. You wouldn't think so, but hacks can be like that. Bad memories for everything but their own specialities. Presumably Val and Phil specialised in fish.

Both claimed they were keen not to cynically rubbish any notion of a miracle in the seafood, but you didn't have to be a genius to see that *The Guardian* would do exactly that. Both would puff the whole business up into some kind of human interest Christmas yarn. They would be hanging out with the workforce, paying for their drinks, or just paying them to say… anything at all. And then *The Sun* would take the piss, or pretend to be mystified, and *The Guardian* would make some fatuous pseudo-sociological point, and then take the piss.

I thought I'd better prepare the staff, so I arranged to speak to the assembled workers during lunch break. Which was how I found myself standing on a table, looking down on this weird bobbling clutch of white-clad people. Suddenly, the notion occurred to me that I had died, and this was heaven, a cold, fishy heaven full of the transformed dead, all clad in angelic raiment. It was like a vision. Something spiritual. But the sight of Alastair's red face reassured me that we were still very much here on earth. He had, he told me, interviewed very member of his workforce, and was still no nearer to finding out who was the secret religious artist. It was clearly preying on his mind. But that was really his problem.

"I'd just like to… I better explain… " I could hear my voice, but it sounded rough, unused, a stranger's. And I realised I had somehow moved from being a hermit in a caravan to addressing a meeting of fish workers on the question of public relations attitudes regarding a piece of salmon emblazoned with a mystical image of the Madonna and child. Possibly, but not probably, by God. Just before Christmas. And this transformation had happened within the space of a week. I felt a smile cross my face.

"Some… some of you will know me. I'm that John Smith from the caravan, the, ah, mad Englishman." There was a smattering of laughter. "Well, you don't have to be mad to work in public relations, but it helps! " More laughter. The old ones are the best. "It certainly helped drive me mad." Silence. Just a bit too far, perhaps.

"Anyway, the thing is, Alastair's brought me in to try and act as a buffer between the firm, between you, and the press. And there are some particularly nasty examples of Her Majesty's hacks on their way, British Airways willing. They'll want to speak to you, and by hook or by crook, they will."

Silence, give or take the sound of plastic cutlery on tin plates, and a low murmuring. Then the measured sound of a male Shetland voice.

"They should be spikkin tae Alastair, and no tae ony o' wis."

"Well," I replied. "They probably will speak to Alastair. But you know, his line is that it's a prank, a joke played by somebody in the factory, and he's trying to find out who. Which he no doubt will. I mean, we can all take a joke, can't we? I don't know which of you has been having a laugh, but at the moment, that's not the point. These reporters want to make the story last. For them it's a Christmas thing."

A different Shetlandic voice came back at me. It was impossible to tell who amongst the 40 or so people there was speaking. Though I could see Alastair peering back through the assembled crowd.

107

"Aye, it's our Christmas bonus too, du sees. We'll tell them anything you want us tae, John. But Alastair'll need to get us some different gelatine if we're to keep this up. That new stuff he got won't hold the dye properly."

There was a murmur of assent.

"No such a good idea in the first place. Could've used cardboard stencils, I think."

"Aye, and the cochineal gets over your fingers."

"We should get more money than we're getting Alastair, and that's a fact. What we're doing is… it's deception. This time the speaker was female, and I could see who it was. A small lass, young with a red tipped nose beneath the white net hat. "It was a laugh at first, and then you just thought you could play it for all it worth, and sell that crap salmon with misprinted boxes. I mean, talk about cheap! Only Alastair Wylie would try and pretend that 'persto' was a Shetland dialect word. When did they ever have pine nuts hereaboots?"

There was a rumbling from the workers, and then, suddenly, the little fishwife-person was up beside me. I was paralysed, flaming faced, embarrassed at my ignorance and stupidity.

"Come on," shouted the girl. "It's time Alastair realised he needs us more than he needs public relations, or a bloody piece of religion on his fish. And blasphemy at that!" She turned directly to the now beetroot-red boss of the company, who was standing, his whole body clenched, in front of her. "Sort out the bonus, Alastair, for all of us. A decent bonus for Christmas. Or we're out of here. And what's more, we'll tell these newspaper fellows exactly what you've been up to." She turned to me, and spoke quietly. "Sorry," she said, and skipped down onto the floor.

I got down myself, shakily. Alastair, his chief salesman, and one of his secretaries remained. As the canteen emptied, I remembered that Shetland possessed almost full employment, and that finding another job would be relatively easy for all these people, if they wanted to. Even just before Christmas. I looked at Alastair, then turned away. He said nothing.

*** *** ***

I settled back into the confines of my cold cottage life, as Christmas approached ever nearer. During my visits to the St Rognvald, the aftermath at Mid-Shetland Seafoods gradually unfolded. Alastair had offered the workers a bigger bonus, if they continued to perpetrate his religious marketing scam. But it didn't make any difference. Freezing fog stopped the two hacks from making it beyond Wick, where they apparently spent two days and nights horizontal in the local British Legion. A bombing outrage in Northern Ireland, just when the peace process seemed locked solid for Yule, then distracted everyone, and despite one of the Madonna and child meals turning up in Crossmaglen, the story was quietly dropped.

"You'll give them their bonus, anyway," I told Alastair, when he turned up at the caravan one icy night with an envelope of cash for me.

"This is for all your trouble," he said. I took it of course. I didn't count it, but I took it. "Aye, I suppose I will give the bastards their Christmas box. Should've told you from the start, but then I thought you'd have guessed. You being a professional... I mean, you couldn't have believed me. Not really?"

"I just didn't think about it, Alastair. I guess I've just stopped being so... just stopped operating on that cynical smartass level. Didn't think it would be... necessary up here."

"Everywhere, pal. You need that everywhere." Alastair stood up to leave. "Look at this bloody Santaland business. Could have told the bloody enterprise idiots that was pure wank right from the start. Have a good Christmas." I shrugged. Christmas.

The truth was, I missed the fluorescent office, the sense of companionship, the camaraderie. Work. And now, even the ridiculous hope of being an Elf had vanished. But of course I'd never go back to Mid-Shetland Seafoods. Not having been made to look that much of a fool. Public relations? Now I could barely relate to myself.

I went back to my lackadaisical life, but it was irksome and hard. Before the brief, embarrassing, so-called job at Mid-Shetland Seafoods, I had been numb, living a robot existence. Now it wasn't enough. I trudged out to the St Rognvald, saw Meena and Ernest, did that drunken conversing thing with the likes of Alf and Vic, started going into Lerwick every week, shopping at the Co-op, and, two weeks before Christmas, put what cash I had left from Alastair's envelope into two envelopes, and sent them off to the boys, along with innocuous, generic Christmas cards. Season's Greetings. No words. I could find no words for what I wanted to say.

I wrote to them, of course. I wrote to them all the time. I just never sent the letters.

I was in the St Rognvald one night, maybe a week before the fateful day, when the phone rang in the bar, and it was for Mister Farrow. I could tell by the way Mel looked at me, arched her eyebrows. Wearily, I nodded, and wandered over to pick up the receiver. I knew who it was. Who it had to be. And sure enough, there was Dorothy, saying hallo, quietly, asking me how things were.

"It's been a year," she said. "I thought you must be… well, I wondered if you were dead. Told the boys you were fine, had gone abroad to… work." Her voice hardened. "I realised you wouldn't have the courage to top yourself."

"I might have died in an accident," I said, quietly as the entire bar studiously tried to appear indifferent while listening acutely to my end of the conversation. "How are the boys, then?"

"They're fine. Few problems at school with... no. No actually, they're not fine at all. They miss you. Or they don't say that, but they do. They need you. I don't. I'd be happy never to see your face again as long as I live. But why did you leave them in the lurch? What did they ever do to you? Why did you do that? At Christmas? "

I said nothing. Then: "You said to go... you said I was... I could..." But I knew. I knew I had left for nobody's good but my own.

"Don't come back," she interrupted. "Do me a favour and don't ever come back. Or if you do, not just some sort of flying visit. I don't care if you don't have a relationship with me, but ... the boys. Duty. Does that mean anything to you? Responsibility? I tell you, it's now or never. Or nothing. Or stay out of their lives forever. Be dead. Just actually be dead." And she put the phone down.

"Merry Christmas," I said, as a pint of Valhalla White Wife appeared in front of me." I'd forgotten to ask if the boys had got their cards.

*** *** ***

In preparation for Christmas Day, I had bought myself some Bernard Matthews turkey burgers and an eccentric selection of alcohol, including the making of several proper, large dry martinis, a very expensive claret and some Champagne, with single-estate rum for afters. It was a self-conscious splurge to push back the darkness, and before the New Year brought its financial and emotional reckoning. There was a need to make money. There was a need to sort things out on every level.

But on Christmas Eve, with a smattering of sleet falling, I made my way to the St Rognvald, where tinsel and crimson decorations abounded, and there was free buffalo chicken wings and chips for the regular drinkers. It was busy, and I wasn't surprised to see some of my former colleagues from Mid-Shetland Seafoods preparing themsleves for the domestic onslaught of the following day by getting absolutely snottered. No Mel, though. She'd be trying to make Christmas special for the wee one, I thought. As you should.

Loud Christmassy country music bellowed from a pair of disco speakers, and a few couples danced where the pool table normally stood. Alastair was there, his face so suffused with blood it was almost a blue-reddy-black, like a three-D bruise.

"How's du?" He shouted, banging me on the back. "That's us all wrapped up for Christmas, then. Pretty good year too. Despite that bloody last minute bonus I had to give them, the bastards."

"No more Madonnas, with or without their youngsters, then?"

He frowned. "No, no we had to abandon that. Falling off in interest. Funny, what with Christmas getting nearer and everything. You'd think... ach. I'm sorry about leading you up the garden path on that one, John. Maybe you'd like to come back after New Year. We need some help in the filleting department."

I shook my head.

"What, painting on Easter bunnies on to cod fillets?" I don't think so, Alastair. Thanks all the same."

Later, somewhat warmed and befuddled, I found myself next to the small woman who had   successfully led the demand for more cash, revealing to me just exactly how deluded I had been.

"I'm sorry," she said. "Would you like to dance?" She was fine-featured, lacking a wedding ring, about 30, I guessed. Elfin.

"I don't... " But she had grabbed my fingers in one of her small calloused hands and was dragging me off my stool. It was dance or tumble.

And we danced. Drank and danced. Ate chicken wings and talked about rubbish. She was a graduate in sociology who had "just come home for a start" after graduating. There was something familiar about her I couldn't quite put my finger on, as if we'd met before, and often. She had been working at Mid Shetland Seafoods for five years, seven years, a lifetime. "Work at the hotel, part time, too, just clearing up. Chambermaid, sort of." She had been married: "Lost the useless chancer to some agricultural implements rep who tried to sell him a tractor. What's a woman doing selling tractors anyway?" No children. Best that way, I almost told her. I stopped myself. No, not better. Not better at all.

At around 11.30 the lights suddenly went out, and the music stopped. Amid the thin blue emergency lights and a babble of voices, someone shouted "Da snow! It's been lying dis past twa hoors." And there was a sudden lunge for the door.

Outside the blackness had been transformed. The air was a swirl of white particles, and drifts were piling up against the hotel door The cars outside were already covered, the edges of the road invisible. There was pandemonium as people rushed back inside to scrabble in the darkness for coats and handbags, and then desperately began clearing snow from their cars. Engines kicked into life, lights blazed. I felt my hand taken by a smaller one.

"Come on," came her voice. And she led me sure-footedly through the darkened, old hotel ghostly in the battery powered emergency lights, past the human shambles of the bar and into the hallway, then up the stairs, three flights. "There's nobody staying tonight," she said. "Though there's bound to be one or two don't get home now. You'd be better here, I think."

She pushed open a bedroom door, and we went into the darkness beyond. As the door closed behind us both, I reached for her, stumbling, unsteady and drunk. But not numbed. Far from that.

"What's... what's your name."

"It's Jennifer," she said.

*** *** ***

I woke, my arm cramped under her. Jennifer was snoring, and I felt as if my head had been used as a punchbag. By an angry kangaroo. A strange dull banging noise seemed to be coming from somewhere. It took several minutes for me to realise my heart wasn't causing it.

The front door was vibrating under the force of blows which had slowed, and yet sounded desperate, when I finally reached it, cold and in bare feet and hastily-hauled-on jeans. No-one but me seemed to be awake at the St Rognvald. I unsnibbed the Yale lock and pulled open one half of the double door, letting in a two-foot drift of snow.

Mel stood there, wrapped in an old duffle coat, with one of those PLO Arab scarfs around her head. She was carrying something. Something... swaddled. Human.

"Johnny," she said. "Thank Christ. I thought I'd never get an answer. The cold water tank in the house has burst. We're flooded out. Me and the bairn."

I opened the door wider, to let the mother and her baby in. The cold air was reviving me a little. I looked at my watch. It was 5 am. It was Christmas morning.

"Merry Christmas, Mel," I said. Her baby began to cry.

Dear Dorothy,

I never thought I'd say this, but it was good to speak to you. It was good to hear your voice.

And so you knew I wasn't dead. You know I'm not. And it was utterly, completely self-centred of me to do what I did. To leave like that, leaving you with such uncertainty.

I know that, I know I can't ask for forgiveness. I don't know where to start asking. Wouldn't know.

But that's what I'm going to do. I'm going to ask for forgiveness. From you. From the boys. I'm going to ask how I can achieve that. What I can do. Short of topping myself, that is. I'm afraid that's no longer an option. I'm looking for kindness. To be kind.

This place. It's a special place. But on the other hand, it could be anywhere, really. Well, no, that's nonsense. But the thing is, it's a community. It's a place where people live together. Are together. Where you can be confident in other people's willingness to live and let live.

It's an island. And you know that stuff about no man being an island, every man's death diminishing me? Well, it's only on an island that you recognise that, realise how true it is. I mean, there are some

real assholes here, and yet, you help
them, are kind to them. Because there you
are, maybe. It's a help-the-asshole kind
of place. And before you say it, yes
that's why they helped me. Why it helped
me. Sure.

I mean, there are folk here who make me
look almost normal. There's the
Shamanistic Shed Couple, who arrived just
a month ago in Volkswagen camper van. They
convinced the crofter at Varga Clett to
rent them an old sheep shed, parked the
van there, and now they're trading
workshops in shamanism for food. Only
thing is, it has to be vegan stuff.

They've got a kid too. Rainbow. About
three. Well looked after, too. Social
workers were round, seemed quite happy.
They're you're clichⅡ crusty hippies, all
stripy jumpers and dreadlocks. She's
Rhiannon, supposedly, and he's, wait for
this, Bombadil. Or Dil for short.

Thing is, the folk, local folk, they're
fine to them. Kind. Give them food. Even
found Dil some work, landscape gardening.

There's Mel, who works at the pub, she's
got a bairn as well. And Victor, Arthur,
Alastair. Jennifer. Someday I'll have to
tell you about Jennifer. Not now.

Things have changed, Dorothy. I've
changed. We need to talk. We need to be
kind. You need to be kind to me, please.

I'll be kind to you. I'll do my best.
Honest. I feel I can. I feel sure I can.

Kindest regards (and I mean it)

Tim

THE RED VAN

SOMETIMES I recognise what ought to be guilt, deep down, frozen up in the glacier I have become.

It's pure ice, clear and glittering, at least some days it is, and I can stare right down into its heart. The two figures are trapped there. Three. Maybe it's three. Still, unmoving. Two. Or three. Two sons and a wife.

I know them. Of course I do. I know the guilt ought to melt me down, reduce this creaky lump of cold solidity to water. Something that could be mopped up, wiped away. Turned to nothing.

Becoming nothing was a possibility, part of the plan, the process of running, moving, going away. Leaving. But that too froze up as I went north, the cold hardening me as I left London far, far behind.

Action is beyond me. I let things happen. I move, like a glacier, slow, infinitesimally slow. Not so as you'd notice. I notice nothing.

Still, I see them, brilliantly illuminated by shafts of sunlight, or shadowed by passing clouds, down, down in my brutally cold heart. I can sense myself wondering, but not caring. Not allowing myself to care.

*** *** ***

In the pub, in the town, in shops, I sometimes hear children's voices:

"Daddy" they say. "Dad."

What is it I feel, some strange knocking, a trapped echo, a splintering?

No. It's nothing.

In the St Rognvald the other day, Bobby o' the Lang Ayre, was telling anyone who would listen about his trip south. Medical treatment. He had to see a consultant in Aberdeen, something about his eyes. He'd never been on a plane before. Eighty if he was a day. It was a great trip for him. Whisked to the airport in a Health Board taxi, on the turboprop to Dyce, bus to the hospital, a night in the Red Cross hospital, then home the next day.

"Ach, me eyes are fading, they say, and I don't fancy an operation. Fine to get the trip, though! See the silver city one last time." He was another former merchant seaman. Maybe he'd never flown, but by God he'd travelled.

He spoke of the delights of Aberdeen, the pub he'd managed to persuade someone to guide him towards, The Prince of Wales ("I mind it well from the old days") and the excitement of flying. But there was one thing he said which hit me so hard I had to leave the bar, a pint drained in a choking hurry.

"There was this boy, wee boy, in a wheelchair, going down, going to the hospital too. And he was crippled mind, all ower da place. Couldna sit right. Jerking a' ower da place. And thin, too. Break your heart. No just thin, but deathly thin. Something bad wrong wi' him. Real bad. Lot o' looking after. And his mam was

119

there, no' old, ken. And she was fussing and helping and wiping
him, and the wee lad couldna speak. Just… sounds, du knows.
Noises.

"Anyway, I'm on the plane, just beside them, across the
corridor, or what ever you call it, and when the engines go for
that take-off, roaring, and the whole tube's just shaking and
shaking… I look over, and the mam is crying, and she's slumped
doon, and the Wee boy, all jerky like, is trying to hold her, but he
can't. He can't. No able, du sees. And then, once we're up, the
wife in charge comes and gives her a wee drink, and says, I
didna ken du wis sae scared. And the mam goes, aye, but you
have to go with the wee yin. And the other wifie looks at the lad,
his hands are all jerking about, and says, you'll need to look
after your mam. And he makes these noises…"

Bobby gazed into his rum and coke. His hand was shaking
slightly.

"Love," he said. And that's when I left.

***　***　***

Bernie had a past. I mean, we all did, all we lost sons and fathers
who washed up on the Zetlandic archipelago. But Bernie had a
serious past.

There were various ways of telling. His accent, for a start,
which was, beneath the deliberate roughening and absorbed
Shetlandic vowels, posh. Posh and used to command, but with
that weird English officer class shyness lurking there. That and
fear. He had eyes which flickered past you all the time. Looking
for something. Or somebody.

Now he drove a van.

"Actually, two vans, old… two vans. Not at the same time,
you ken. I suppose, the thing is, I have two vans."

We were in the St Rognvald. Bernie had arrived in Shetland

some seven years previously, apparently just another Englishman with equity realised from a house sale south, and a desire to downshift. He lived just south of Grunnawick, in a croft house called Sodom. I'd seen it from the road. Up on a little rise, obviously with money spent on it. Presumably the van thing was just to add to the bank interest. I'd joked about the name, pillars of salt, and was told that Sodom was quite a common Shetland name. It came from the Norse, Sudheim, or South House.

He had a wife and two kids in their teens, all nice, normal, friendly, well integrated. But there was something about Bernie. He was quiet, reserved. The occasional pint in the bar, friendly but aloof. Alf claimed he had once seen him break a drunken Norwegian's thumb when the visiting fisherman started fondling Brenda, one of the local girls.

"Just as if he was saying hallo. Smiling, went to the guy to shake hands. Next minute, the Norski's blubbering on the floor, screaming. Big fellow too. And Bernie's just walking away, as if nothing happened."

Alf had shaken his head in admiration. He was a connoisseur of applied violence. There were rumours that Bernie was some kind of mercenary, or a police informer. Ex-forces, anyway. But nobody had asked him outright about his past. That wasn't the way.

Now I was sitting next to Bernie, feeling twinges in my hands.

"I have twa... two vans," he said. "And too much work really. Besides, I don't want to be going to the terminal ower... too much. And there's a big new contract on there. Pipework replacement. They've had me running in and out to Lerwick, one of the contractors. I could do with someone to help me out, frankly. Reasonable money. Cash in hand, if you like."

It sounded better than doing PR for Mid-Shetland Seafoods and the Virgin Mary, that was for sure.

The van was an old Mercedes 207 diesel, red, like nearly all Shetland's panel vans. Everywhere else, it was white van man. Here it was red. Something to do with the salt-fuelled rust, I suspected, which invaded everything metallic left exposed to the fast-moving sea-air. Red showed less of it than white.

"I've got a Transit 35 hundredweight," said Bernie. "Better for some things. Bales of hay. Got this as a spare. You can, ah, drive?"

"Clean licence. Well, apart from three points for speeding, years ago. And I think that's lapsed."

"Can I see it?" I was reaching for my wallet automatically when my hand froze.

"I think I've left it at home, Bernie," I said, retrieving my hand.

"But I am licensed. Not disqualified. Nothing to worry about."

"It's just…" and his tone was apologetic, even if his eyes were, for once steady on mine. "Insurance."

I shrugged. "Bernie, maybe this job isn't such a good idea."

He smiled. A huge, charming smile which transformed his face completely.

"Oh, look, John. Tim. Timothy. I know about your… other life, your past if you will. We all have pasts. You might be surprised how many people hereabouts know all about you. Phone calls to the St Rognvald, that sort of thing. And besides…" His gaze dropped to his feet. "Sorry. I… ah, called somebody I know. Who sort of knows you. Or of you." He raised his eyes, looked at me and beyond me. The voice lost its veneer of Shetlandic. "The fact that you have, well, something to hide, and that in the end of the day it's fairly innocent, or

122

innocent enough from at the very least an insurance company point of view, is actually… I find it quite reassuring."

I felt a weird mixture of relief and anger. "What gives you the right? What's your big secret, anyway, Bernie. People say… "

"I know what people say, John. And it is John, as far as I'm concerned. And they're all wrong. They're all wrong. Do you have that licence?"

I took out my wallet and handed the worn mush of pink paper to him. He unfolded the licence and looked at it.

"You need to change your address on this, John. And if you're serious, the name too. I could help you there, if you want. If you're sure."

I took the licence back. "I'm not sure," I said. I didn't feel angry anymore. Or curious. Or anything much.

The red Mercedes van had power steering, and while the single-track roads around Grunnawick had me cursing stray sheep, bad fencing or the illegal grazing of flocks on verges, it was relatively easy to handle. On a motorbike, if you hit a sheep, you were most likely dead. In the Stuttgart solidity of the Merc, it was thinly-sliced mutton and a bit of wool in the radiator grille.

It was winter, winter waiting for the first glimmer of spring. Still dark in the afternoons, still light deprivation central. But I had Jennifer, and something within me was shifting, crunching, like pack ice, globally-warmed.

I was running crated gear almost daily to one of the contractors at the terminal, which crouched like an ashamed city south east of Grunnawick, massive, hulking, with its flarestacks lending an orange pulse to the night sky, or smoking in a sinister fashion during the day. Tankers, both gas and oil came in to pick up loads, or in the case of one, to bring oil in from a field called Schiehallion, out in the Atlantic and in water too deep for any pipeline to exist. I couldn't imagine what life was like out on an oil platform. And in the Atlantic fields, there were no rigs, no solid legs locked onto the seabed. Just a converted tanker swinging about at the whim of satellite positioning.

Getting into the terminal was a joke, really. There was still loads of equipment being liberated form the site, even though the workforce had shrunk from the 7000 of its seventies peak to a mere 700 or so. And if you needed anything made – pipework, a flue for your Rayburn – the engineering workshops would do the business, at a price.

"All right, Johnny Boy?" It was Edgar, the front gate security officer, squawking electronically as I waited at the barrier. "On you go in." And I was through, driving along narrow roadways between banks of pipes and humming machinery.

Coming out that wind-buffeted, uneasily stormy day was different, though. Just as I arrived at the exit, and was leaning over to catch Edgar's eye and be waved on, a siren started a series of howling yelps. Edgar visibly jumped, and I could see him picking up a phone. He spoke for a few moments, then put the receiver down and sat gazing down at his desk. I blipped the Merc's horn. He jerked his head, saw me and raised the barrier, waving me out, saying nothing.

I was heading back up to Grunnawick when I saw Bernie's Transit coming in the opposite direction. He flashed his lights, and we stopped abreast of each other. I wound down my window.

"Back up," he said, for the first time gazing straight at me and holding the look. "Follow me. There's something you should see."

I followed Bernie down the winding side road which leads to the village of Sullom, on the other side of Sullom Voe from the oil terminal bearing that name. We drove past an abandoned quarry, then down a rough track to a massive concrete pier which looked as if was rarely used. When our engines stopped,

I could still hear the terminal's emergency siren, echoing faintly across a quarter mile of seawater.

"This is called Gaza," said Bernie, walking out to the end of the jetty. "Used in the war. They used to have Sunderland flying boats over there. And for the quarry when it was working. They got stone from here for building the terminal." He laughed quietly. "I heard about one man who worked at the quarry, got some stone fragments in an eye. Guy who told me, old crofter, broad as you like, think he'd never read a book in his life, said to me, aye boy, eyeless in Gaza."

"Samson," I said. "It was Samson who had his eyes put out in Gaza. Then he pulled down the entire temple on top of the Philistines."

"Durrell was what this old boy had been reading," said Bernie thoughtfully. "He would have known the Samson reference, but he probably thought it was too obvious." He shook his head. "That's Lawrence Durrell, not Gerald, by the way. Never could stand those bloody animal books. Anyway, take a look at that."

He was pointing at what seemed at first a typical Sullom Voe scene. In the short winter afternoon, the water was lumpy, steel grey beneath a fast-moving, cloudy sky. A couple of shags laboured by, black and goose-like. A seal popped its doghead out of the water and peered at us from under long supermodel eyelashes. Night was already in the air. A tanker was being shepherded into one of the jetties by two tugs, while one of the fire control boats stood by. Everything seemed to be happening very slowly, as it usually did ."See how low she is in the water? Hardly any leeway at all. She's full of oil, heading out, and they're pushing her back in."

"Why's that?" Bernie was rummaging in the cab of his Transit, and emerged with a pair of Leitz binoculars. He peered through them at the ship, then handed them to me.

"No fire, at least that's something. Nothing much to see for now, but there will be. There will be, you can bloody bet on it." He was muttering fiercely. "Now we'll see. Now we'll see just how effective their bloody environmental protection plans are."

All I could see through the binoculars was a close-up version of what I already knew was there: a tanker. Tugs. Another emergency boat standing by.

"What is it, Bernie? What's happened?" He had turned his back and was heading back to the vans.

"She's holed. Holed below the waterline. Single-skin hull, clobbered the mid-channel rocks on the way out. The *Hydrocarbon Valdez*, Panama registered. Panama." He shook his head scornfully. "Some multinational shithead company, never find out who really owns it. Paper maze. Bastards. Anyway, hit those rocks, the baas as they call them. Which is almost impossible, if you're not pissed or asleep. Must have lost power and drifted before the tugs could get to her. Big tide two hours ago. Bad wind. Crap crew. Something went wrong, anyway." I had never seen him so agitated. "Now all we can do is wait and see. Come on. I'll give you a drink."

We went back to his house. To Sodom. His wife Mary was peeling tatties when we arrived. She looked solemn.

"How bad is it?"

"Don't know." Bernie folded his arms and sighed. "The morning will tell. John and I are going to have a drink. Maybe I'll give Ron a phone. See what's happening." The only Ron I had heard of was the Chief Inspector in Lerwick, Ronald "Birch 'em" Macgillivary. I couldn't imagine how Bernie knew him. Or maybe I could.

"Don't call him, Bernard. He'll be busy. Wait and get the Radio Shetland news at half-five. They'll know." Mary turned to me. She was a neat woman, late forties and fit, with a weathered face just a notch shy of beautiful. "Stay for supper, John. The

126

kids… the kids are in Lerwick. Some badminton thing." I couldn't miss the hesitation. I hesitated too. But suddenly the Scraada croft seemed a lonely place to be. Me sitting and writing, writing. Writing into the void. Calling into the abyss. Jenny was a just a walk away, sure.

It was the mention of children that did it. I was sort of glad Bernie and Mary's kids weren't there, to be honest. But I liked being close to their absence. I liked the sense of parenthood that was palpable at Sodom.

Maybe guilt is a luxury. Maybe all this numbness is just displaced self-pity, another example of my surpassing selfishness. Maybe that's what men do. Run and hide, hide and run.

The ice is cracking and shifting, though. Or the thaw is coming. Maybe it's Jennifer. Maybe not

Something happened the other day, a weird thing. I was round at Ali's house, Ali a sort of washed-up hippy who dabbles in ceramics and majors in growing dope. Not that I was buying. I was just delivering a couple of cartons which probably contained seeds. A lot of seeds.

Anyway, playing on Ali's ancient, massive, vinyl-only hi-fi was The Grateful Dead, a band I have always sneered at. It was some live bootleg thing from the seventies, and the swooning, stoned quality of the meandering jams had a kind of period charm. Then they began to sing.

And they can't really sing, the Dead, not really. They're crap, all of them. Garcia, Hunter, Lesh. When they try and do that Crosby Stills and Nash thing, they veer crazily around the notes, harmonies wonky, a ripped smile audible on every face.

But one set of words howled tunelessly out at me. Lodged in my head.

"All we can do," they sang, "is forgive. And try to be kind."

And as I turned down a toke on Ali's joint, sipped at weird-

tasting hippy tea, I could feel the breath of some warm wind rippling across the ice field inside me. Kind. Kindness. People were naturally kind, some of them at least. I wasn't. I was naturally tense, cynical, generally malcontent.

But kindness was good. I liked kindness. I responded to it. And the fact was that nearly everybody in Shetland tried to be kind. Even the least naturally inclined that way. Because that's what it took to live here. To get along with other people. To survive in an environment which could blow you off your feet and the roof off your house. Where the sea could pluck whole families of breadwinners from their boats. Where black gold could turn to a foul suppurating black tide, and sweep evil and destruction on land and sea, creatures and vegetation, you and your neighbours' inheritance. To be kind was necessary. For some, and for some of the time for everyone, kindness was an act of will.

Try to be kind. Forgive. Forgive? Forgive who? I was the one who had done all the bad stuff. And no-one was going to forgive me, were they?

Music, said Bernie, weaving back into the room from the sound of a flushing toilet, and heading for his immaculate collection of CDs.

"Any Grateful Dead?" I asked. He looked at me in amazed horror.

"I was thinking more Dire Straits, myself." Suddenly Bernie's face tautened. I thought I could detect white around his lips. "I hate the druggy shit," he said. "Hate it. You don't take drugs, do you, Tim? John?" His fists were clenched. Quite suddenly, I felt vaguely threatened.

I grinned carefully, deliberately. "Dire Straits," I said. "Why not? Always loved that guitar sound."

"Good choice," said Bernie. "Money for nothing, and your chicks for free."

"Quite."

***   ***   ***

We were still drunk next morning. A bottle and a half of prime whisky had been sunk, and both us were feeling the effects. And looking the worse for it. Mary hadn't touched a drop. She didn't have a face like thunder. Not exactly. More a sort of general depression over Iceland.

"Coffee," she told me. I had slept on the couch, in my clothes. "Bernie'll be through in a moment. When he's stopped being sick."

It was good coffee. Strong enough to stick your gums to your cheeks. A mug each and we were on our way, groggy, wavering a little on what was, at 9 am, an icy road, with only a glimmer of daylight in the east. Bernie switched on the radio. It was on the national news. We were. Our island. Our home. Made it sound remote, though: Damaged tanker. Oil spill. A thousand barrels.

"Is that a lot?"

"Not in the grand scheme of things." Bernie grimaced as a sheep wandered into our path and the van swerved. "Not in a storm. Not in the open sea. On Gluss Ayre, in one seal colony, it's a slaughter."

At Gaza, there were five or six vehicles parked by the pier, including Carrie's library van, and a small crowd staring out over the water. In the growing daylight I recognised faces I knew: Alf. Dodie Two Hats. Alastair was there, even Mel, for God's sake, her infant huddled close. She was standing near Alf. Too near to be casual. Good grief. Victor was there too. A couple of pairs of binoculars passed from hand to hand. There was a

129

strong smell of fuel oil in the air. A sense of… grief. Bad grief.

Greetings were murmured. There were no jokes. And as I looked down from the pier on the little shingle beach next to it, I could see why. It was black. The stench of fuel was suddenly overwhelming. More shocking was the fact that the thick coating on the stony shore, above the receded tide, was, in places, moving sluggishly. A black wing reared with terrible slowness. A ruined, dying otter tried to haul itself above the dark hydrocarbon slime. Along with the slow rustle of the waves and the murmuring of the wind, I could head Mel sobbing. My own throat felt choked, blocked. It was hard to swallow. The chemical pricking at my eyes had me blinking back tears. Or maybe it was the wind.

"Can we help?" I turned to Bernie in what seemed like desperation, just as a police car pulled up, it blue light conspicuously off, its siren silent.

"No." He shook his head. He'd been talking to Alf, who pursed his lips in agreement.

"Leave it to the sea and the wind," he said. "All we can do. It's a fucking tragedy, but it could be worse. There's no major seal or otter colonies along here, and we're out of the bird breeding season. A few sheep'll eat the oil and die, but that serves the fuckers right. Less sheep the better, in my view."

"You won't find many agreeing with you." The voice was Highland, used to authority. I turned to find a policeman, clad in yellow reflective jacket, obviously senior. I breathed in, trying to disguise the whisky reek on my breath. Though it was Bernie who had been driving. "Hallo Bernie. How's things?"

Bernie grinned, shook the copper's hand warmly. "Hi Ron. What's the story?"

"Pumped the oil out of the holed tank, divers are patching her. Thousand barrels, give or take. They've contained most of it, soaked up some. This is the worst of it. Can't complain really.

130

Could have been worse. The Cruelty people'll be along in a minute. Might try and do something for the birds. But best put them out of their misery, I think."

"Yes." Bernie sniffed the air. "Might burn, though. Start a fire with some petrol, we could clean it up that way. What do you think, Ron? Victor?"

Victor shook his head. "No. Not bunker fuel. Too thick and slimy and anyway, it's wet. A bomb might do it. Napalm or something. But there's not much. No, Leave it to nature. There's a big wind coming this afternoon. There'll be stuff left. It'll harden on the rocks. There's places where bunker oil came ashore during the war, torpedoed merchantmen, and it's still there, hard as the rock itself, but black. The bad stuff'll go. It'll be gone tomorrow. Mark my words."

People were drifting back to their cars. I saw the chief inspector hold Bernie's arm and mutter something into his ear. Bernie nodded, half-smiled.

"What was he saying to you?" We were back in the van, warming up with the engine as we drove slowly north.

"Told me to try and find some polo mints, Bernie said sombrely. "Better I think, if we have a quick early pint. Mel'll open the bar for us at the St Rognvald. She and Alf are heading there now. Then peppermints. Maybe."

We stayed in the St Rognvald all day, and as the drinking wore on, the wind rose. By the time night fell again, around 3.00 pm, there was howling gale, with gusts of sleet battering the hotel windows. Jennifer was there, not looking tremendously impressed, probably. I was in no condition to notice. But she took me home, and dragged me to bed, where she proceed to have her wicked way with me. Approximately. I was dimly pleased with myself for being able to perform something akin to the dirty deed.

I slept in next day. We both did. It was past noon by the time

I struggled on foot up to Sodom with the keys for the red van. The place was still as the grave, shuttered and asleep. I drove carefully down to Gaza.

The storm had eased. The awful smell of fuel had vanished. Most of the beach had been scoured clean. Black bunker oil still clung to some rocks above the tide line, but it was as if God had wiped the place up, angrily, disgusted with what his creatures had done. Leaving some marks behind as a warning of what might have been.

There was a voice behind me. I turned to find Chief Inspector MacGillivary behind me once more.

"You shouldn't sneak up on people."

"Why not? It's what I'm supposed to do." Then he laughed, clapped me on the shoulder. "Alfred was right, eh? Mostly gone."

"Yeah."

"People here, they pretend they're hard," he said. "Not like the Hebrides, where I come from. They're a lot softer there on the outside. Gentler, and then when you get inside, messed up with religion. Here it's all hard, fierce on the outside. But God, they're soft-hearted. The idea of animals dying because of that oil. It was killing some of the men who were here yesterday, despite what they might say. Despite some of the salmon farmers among them shooting all the seals they can. It's like the land and the sea are a part of them, and if some... alien force comes and taints it, it's like a disease in their own bodies. An infection."

"Have we met, before, Chief Inspector?"

"Call me Ron. No, we haven't. Though obviously I've heard about you. And Bernie asked me to make sure you weren't some international jewel thief. Or a paedophile."

"And you're... friends? You and Bernie... Ron."

"Well, yes, I suppose we are." The inspector began to walk

back to his fluorescent yellow Land Rover Defender. "But we were colleagues, in a manner of speaking. If we'd ever met at the time, that is. He probably hasn't told you, has he? He was the youngest assistant chief constable in Britain at one point. Cambridgeshire force. Resigned. Left under a bit of a cloud."

"Oh really?"

"Yes" he said. "Drunk driving. Then he made the mistake of planting the officious young policeman who arrested him. Bad, that. Loss of control. Hushed it up of course. Violent sod, Ron, when he loses his temper. Was known for it, they say. Not a man to cross. Decided to drop out of the mainstream. Mary, I think. Came here. Drives a van. Stays sober, most of the time." And with that, he climbed into his Land Rover and started the rattly diesel up. He wound down the window and leaned out. "And your breath could kill a seal quicker than any oil pollution, son. Get some mints, for goodness' sake. Before you run into a policeman."

Scoured clean. Scrubbed by the wind and the waves, and the action of salt and gritty sand. But with the eternal, always solidifying mark of where the pollution had been. Left as a sign. A reminder. A warning.

A stain.

I was in Domestic Supplies in Lerwick the other day, looking for a chair. Just a comfortable chair, or maybe a small sofa. Something cheap. But there was this beautiful leather recliner, one of those things you can tilt back and which has a platform for your feet. Just the thing for snoozing in before the Rayburn or the telly, or both.

So I sat in it. And one of the salesmen, Nicky, I think his name is, came up and said he would let me have it cheap.

"Reduced from £800," he said. "You can have it for five."

"Bit beyond me, Nicky, even at five hundred." I stretched out luxuriantly.

"It was only six weeks she had it," Nicky said thoughtfully, "when he popped his clogs. Died right there in it. Painless, they think. He was eighty. Old Philip of Voursta Clag. Made his cash in livestock shipping. Only minimal staining, Cleaned up very nicely, I think. Four hundred, then, to you. And fifty."

I gingerly pulled myself out of the chair's leathery depths, feeling a weird prickling along my spine. I looked at the smooth upholstery, But I couldn't see any sign of human stains too horrible to even imagine. But then, it's hard to to see stains on black.

I walked down the street, feeling as if death was stuck to my back like Velcro. At Leask's travel agents, I stopped for a while, and gazed at the offers in the window: Tenerife, from Aberdeen, £400 for a fortnight. Bermuda. The Gambia. Change your life, Tim, something whispered deep in my head. Change it. Move away. Go somewhere else. Lose yourself. There's a whole world out there.

Then I walked in and booked a flight to Heathrow. A return.

Dear Billy and Jerry,

This is your father here.

I've written to you before. I don't mean
the cards at Christmas. I've written
letters, lots of them. Quite a few, anyway.
Most of them I threw away or burnt
immediately I was finished. One or two I
kept. Maybe someday you'll see them.

I want to send this one. This is not
about me. It's about you. It's for you. And
if your mum sees it, that's OK. Show it to
her. Maybe she'll see it first, decide if
you should have it. Maybe I'll send it to
her first.

I want to come and see you. I'm
frightened about that. Scared to leave the
island, scared of what lies down there in
that big place they call here "Sooth".
South. And I'm frightened of seeing you. Of
what you might say, and of what your mum
will say. I'm scared of what you won't say,
of you not wanting to see me.

I wondered if I should write to you, sort
of man to man, and ask straight out if you
wanted to see me or not. Take your decision
on it. But I think, in the end of the day,
that's a bit of a cop out on my part. I
think it's time for me to be a man. It's
time for me to stop running away. Stop
being lost.

I want to be your father. No, that's not

right. I am your father. The genes, the DNA...they're your mum's and mine. Maybe I'm talking crap. Maybe I'm just reassuring myself. But I met a man the other day, a lovely man. He and his wife fostered, then adopted three children, all very young, toddlers or babies. Brought them up well, treated them equally. Now he's old. How are his kids, I asked him.

"They're fine," he said, "but I'll tell you an interesting thing. They all became their parents."

What, I said, they all turned out like you?

"Well, no. They all followed the paths their birth parents took. In a good way. I think we gave them the good stuff, the good direction. Comfort and security. But they became their parents. One had some oil rig roustabout for a dad, useless piece of travelling trash. A 19-year-old trainee nurse for a mother. He's a doctor, seconded to BP, travelling the world setting up medical care for oil workers. Looking for his bloody dad, being his mum."

It may be rubbish, but I cling to that. And there's stuff you need to know. That knowing me will maybe help you deal with. You don't want to turn out like me, but maybe that stupid DNA is already hurtling you down that path.

Maybe that's part of what being a father

is. Just being around so your kids can watch and learn and avoid the pitfalls you found yourself in.

I think it would be worthwhile for us to at least know each other. I think there's things I could give to you. I know there's an infinite amount you could give me. I can feel the loss, now, your loss, in a way I never could before.

But that's me again. Me. And as I said before, this is about you.

I have a job, sort of. It's not a great job, but there's a little money. I'll help you all I can. But it's not the money. It's about trying to learn how to be a father. To find out what that means for me and you.

As for this place, maybe I will leave. Or maybe I can't. Boys, I wish I could show it you. The winters which close the whole island into itself, where the darkness hides a weird human warmth. The summer days which sometimes never turn to night. The people. And there are great swimming pools, though I've never been in one of them. All that money from oil. Boats. Fishing. Good things. Good stuff.

It's home, I suppose, now for me. It's brought me back to life. Remember that stupid old gospel preacher we used to see in the mall, how we used to laugh at him? Or I did, sometimes, when I came to get you at weekends. On the odd weekend. And I'm sorry about that, too. The way I looked,

and maybe smelt sometimes. I still take a
drink, But I'm not like that anymore.
Honest.

Anyway, that preacher. He had a billboard
he propped up in front of him, him with his
frayed nylon shirt and and his drinker's
nose, all broken red veins. Remember?
Remember what it said on that piece of
cardboard? I Once Was Lost, but now am
fownd." Fownd, with a w. You laughed. I
laughed. Bad spelling. But actually, it was
old English, from some old edition of the
Bible. Fownd.

I'll be down in about a fortnight. Please
be kind to me. I know I don't deserve it.

Love

Dad

Dorothy, I'm sending this to you, because
I realise I haven't written it in a way the
boys could easily understand, or at least
parts of it. Can you translate it for them?
I think I can depend on you to do that.
I'll see you a week on Friday, weather
permitting.

Best,
Tim

ARRIVAL

It was late April. Spring. Green shoots were appearing, but there was snow in the air. And on the air, too: The BBC had been bellowing warnings all morning about a depression over Norway, easterly winds bearing huge quantities of white nastiness. Shetland could fuck you up like that, just when you though the dark days of winter were over.

I woke late, with my heart pounding. There was a note from Jenny on the kitchen table, saying she'd had to go to work early. The Rayburn was still warm, and I clanked open the vents before filling the firebox with dry wood and peat.

The house was tidy. Clean as it would ever be. The previous night, Jenny and I had brushed and dusted and sprayed and polished and washed. There had always been two old single beds, hand-carved out of driftwood, in the ben-end room on the first floor. I'd bought two mattresses at Home Furnishings in Lerwick, duvets, sheets. Towels.

Furnishing a home. My home. Not ours yet, not Jenny's and mine. But maybe. Just maybe.

I'd borrowed an old Toyota Hi-Lux from Alf, his second best-one, he said. Bernie would have let me have a van, but the Merc was off the road, and the he needed the Transit for a North

Roe run. The Hi-Lux smelt vaguely of fish and tar, but was relatively respectable. at least, after two hours using the Powerwasher and Vacu-Car in Brae it was. After washing my mug, listening one last time to the bad weather news, I shut the door and headed down the track to the tattered Japanese pick-up.

It was a crew-cab, the one with four seats. There was dog there, I realised, in addition to the tar and fish, despite extensive cleaning and the presence of four of those perfume sachets you buy in garages. Maybe I'd accidentally bought dog and fish perfume ones, specially designed for homesick Shetland crofters.

It started in a rattle of blue diesel smoke, and I headed south. The plane was due in at noon, and it would take me an hour to get to Sumburgh from Grunnawick.

No snow, yet. Just a heavy, glowering sky and the kind of edgeless cold you get before the flakes start falling. I shook the bad thoughts away. The plane would make it. I would make it.

The St Rognvald's lunchtime traffic jam was beginning as I puttered past, I glimpsed Mel as the door swung open to admit Alf and Bernie. Bernie waved. Alf wagged his finger: take care of my beautiful, expensive piece of shit, he was saying. Was that Jenny's shadow I caught in one of the upstairs windows, going about her housemaidenly duties? Probably just wishful thinking. I spotted Alastair drawing up, still in his white fish-factory coat. Victor would be along soon, Dodie Two-Hats, maybe. I felt a brief pang of thirst. Of neediness.

The oil terminal loomed in the west, the flare stacks burning, setting the sky a-shimmer. Biggest in Europe, yet all of a piece with the landscape, huddling and hunkered down into the grey and brown. No trace now of the holed tanker *Hydrocarbon Valdez*. I knew there were still deep residues of bunker fuel on the rocks along Sullom Voe. But the word from the almighty Scottish Natural heritage, the RSPB and other god-like quangos, was that the Valdez spill was going to have "no significant impact on the immediate environment." I still felt my gut lurch thinking about it. But we would see. Sometimes the sea could be merciless. And sometimes forgiving.

Mid-Shetland Seafoods appeared after a while, steaming gently through its stainless steel chimney. They were doing quite well, apparently. Buying some organic salmon. Selling it fresh and plain, no additives, no funny stuff. I settled into the rhythm of the fast road from Brae southwards, passing the gorgeous little postcard village of Voe, where they made the jumpers worn by Sir Edmund Hilary and his Everest team. Past the turn-off to Lunna, where the legendary Shetland Bus operation helped saved Norway during World War Two. The featureless waste of the Lang Kames, then the vast sweep of salmon farms at Wadbister. Sandloch. The little lake, with its curiously yellow, sandy shore, surrounded with sinister legends about bodies disposed of during meat smuggling operations in the war. It didn't do to talk too much about that, even now.

I bypassed Lerwick, sweeping right at the golf course as the sky continued to darken. But by Cunningsburgh, there was a lightening on the horizon, I was sure of it. I checked the radio again: doom, gloom. Snow.

Sumburgh Airport is a massive white elephant, a gigantic remnant of the oil industry's halcyon days. Most of the huge terminal is unused, with the helicopter operations to the North Sea and Atlantic platforms moved away to cheaper, smaller airstrips. Now, every incoming British Airways flight attracts a gaggle of taxi drivers and relatives, who rattle about in the building like crumbs in a biscuit tin.

We gathered more in hope for Flight BA8767 from Aberdeen, Glasgow and, long, long ago, via some oilman's shuttle express, London. No BA staff could be seen, and there were no announcements saying it was going to be delayed. The

141

monitors hanging from the ceiling just said "arrival expected, 11.59." By 12.05, there was nothing.

"Bound to snow," said Francis, a taxi driver I vaguely knew of, due to his alleged dealing in illicit Russian vodka and cigarettes, brought ashore from the Mafia-owned factory ships which still occasionally called at Lerwick. "Don't know what it's like in Aberdeen. Coming from the Bloody Norskies."

I peered out of the window facing out over the main runway. Could anything fly in that? Of course it could. Couldn't. Could. And then, out of the swirling heaviness of the clouds, a black, wobbly speck appeared. Simultaneously, a deep droning whirr filled my ears. I felt a huge weight lift off my chest.

Still no announcement. But I could see the long shape of the ATP (Advanced Turbo Prop, or Another Technical Problem as they say in Shetland) beginning to disgorge its passengers. Were they there? It was too far away to tell.

*** *** ***

I remembered my flight south, just a few weeks previously. The mist clearing to reveal a propeller-driven plane straight out of that last scene in *Casablanca*. Climbing in, hearing the engines splutter into life, roar and then settle into a huge, vibrating hum. The taxiing to the end of the runway, then the build-up of power in the engines as the pilot revved them against the brakes. Everything shaking, luggage compartment doors opening above my head. Then the shove in the back as the brakes were released, a sort of slow trundling, picking up speed, until finally that lurch into the air. And I realised that flying had hardly changed since the Wright Brothers. It was still a human insult against gravity. Against God.

We climbed, banked, and I looked out and back, to the sea thrashing white against the rock, at a sweep of fake-looking golden sand, at the browny green of peatbog, dotted with the golfball shapes that were sheep. We passed over a lobster boat, wallowing in the tidal race off Sumburgh Head. Da Roost. It sparkled, the boat, with fresh paint. New boats, old rocks, I thought. Alf had said that to me when Victor had started talking about having a new boat built for him, a so-called Shetland Model, a Viking design, which to my eyes was basically pointed at both ends. New boats, old rocks.

The plane landed at Aberdeen, then took off again for Glasgow, where I transferred to a jet. Heathrow was as I remembered it, a choking gaggle of desperate and hopeful people, policemen with machine guns. I felt panic rising in my throat, an ache for the space and calmness and big bad weather of Shetland. But I fought it down, and began looking for signs to the Underground.

*** *** ***

The electric door slid open, and the straggle of people began making landfall among their loved ones, their business connections, their captors: One man in handcuffs was handed over to two plain-clothes cops. Smartly-dressed executives headed for Bolts' car hire desk. Suddenly, I wondered what I looked like: I'd dressed up for my visit south, for that heartrending, terrifying… reunion was the wrong word. For my meeting with Dorothy. With Will. With Gerald. I'd looked maybe thinner, bonier. It had been weird, putting on a proper shirt, thinking about a tie. Clothes had been nothing to me but practical protection against cold and wet, for months.

Now they were coming, and what did I have on? What on earth did I have on? Battered but well polished Tufftrak steel-toed boots; jeans. A Dickies fleece and a brutally-blue Shetland Fair Isle sweater Jenny had given me as a joke. "Mak' dee look

143

lik a Whalsay purser skipper, only withoot the money." That and a woollen Dexy's Midnight Runners (circa Geno) hat.

At least I'd shaved.

Suddenly I thought of how I'd looked when I left them, putting on that motorcycle helmet, tucking my face away for the long, longest journey into oblivion. I'd had one of those de rigueur goatees, styled hair, not the long straggly stuff peeping out, grey from beneath my bunnet. And I'd been heavier by maybe two stone. Fat. Fat and weak.

They materialised in front of me, invading my dreams, my fears. Bigger, more adult, somehow, in this context. In the bare fluorescent airport light. Jerry with a deep voice.

"Hi Dad." He was offering me his hand to shake. I took it, awkwardly. For the first time, I saw myself in him, in the cast of his eyes. Billy was hanging back slightly. Lingering half in, half out of his brother's bulk.

"Hi Bill," I said. "Welcome to the Shetland Islands."

"Hi," he said.

Nothing else was said, as we moved over to the conveyor to pick up their luggage. There would be time for talking. Later. I hoped.

"Best get a move on, " I said. "It looks like snow."

"In April?" Jerry was incredulous. "The trees have leaves in London."

"No trees, here, pal." then I added, hastily. "Well, not as many as you're used to. The wind, and... everything."

"Is it far?" Billy's voice for the first time. Slightly tremulous.

"Quite a long way," I replied. "Quite a long way."

A word on Shetland Dialect: I would have been utterly at sea without the generous and unstinting help of Vaila Wishart, editor of *The Shetland Times* and my sometime boss, in modifying my tenuous grasp on Shetlandic. I apologise in advance for any outrage caused to dialect purists but I think even they would agree that most dialect speakers shift back and forth between Scots-English and Scots-Norse as the demands of their listeners dictate.

I have tried to make the meaning of essential dialect words apparent through their usage in the book. Have I made it clear that the Simmer Dim is Shetland's midsummer "midnight sun"? I hope so. 'ESA' is not dialect, though it is a term widely heard in rural Shetland. Payments to crofters for keeping certain fields as "Environmentally Sensitive Areas" are crucial to many people's incomes.

My special thanks to Vaila for her editing skills, and to Charlotte Black for commissioning the book in the first place. Two chapters have appeared previously, in different form, in *The Shetland Times*, and some small sections had their origins in pieces written for *The Scotsman* and for BBC Radio Scotland. Thanks to Ricky Ross for the book's title — check out the wonderful album *New Recording* for the original song — and to Rab McNeill for guidance on the further/farther debate.

None of the characters in this book are real. It is a work of fiction. Well none of the characters save Shetland itself. It is real all right. Gloriously so, and as much of a salvation for me as it was for Timmy Farrow.

Tom Morton
Shetland, August 2003

I Want You To Hurt Like I Do
By Randy Newman. Published by Warner Brothers Music.